PRAISE FOR
THE EL PASO RED FLAME GAS STATION
(SHORT STORIES) BY
J. REEDER ARCHULETA

"A well-wrought panorama of small-town dramas and discontents."

—KIRKUS REVIEWS

"A boy growing up alone in a hardscrabble Texas town weathers poverty, violence, and heartbreak in this coming-of-age saga. Archuleta's (Rio Sonora, 2010, etc.) tense stories unfold like chapters in a novella about a boy named Josh struggling to make his way in the 1950s and 60s...colorful and charismatic characters...Josh's town is convincingly crafted from punchy, plainspoken dialogue... The result is an atmospheric Texas bildungsroman reminiscent of Larry McMurtry's *The Last Picture Show.*"

"...Thoroughly engaging..."

— THE CLARION REVIEW

"...Narrated with passion and eloquence...Themes of dealing with loss, death, and love are captivating...Intimate understandings of the settings are evident in the depth of the descriptions and the emotional content of each story. True-to-life dialogue...Archuleta's collection offers poignant and hopeful stories of determination in the face of need."

"...A lovingly rendered portrait of a Texas life..."

— BLUE INK REVIEW

"The stories are conveyed in lean, elegant prose reminiscent of Annie Proulx and Cormac McCarthy...The novella succeeds on multiple levels...Archuleta's characters are captivating: wise but never preachy, weary but not cynical...the world they reside in is sublimely rendered through expertly selected details...Archuleta's ability to distill a story to its raw elements brings a weight and depth belied by its brevity...a timeless quality...Any lover of literary fiction, or anyone simply hungry for a good book, is sure to find sustenance in Archuleta's prose."

THE EL PASO RED FLAME

THE
EL PASO RED
FLAME
GAS STATION

AND OTHER STORIES

J. REEDER ARCHULETA

IZZARD INK
PUBLISHING

IZZARD INK PUBLISHING
PO Box 522251
Salt Lake City, Utah 84152
www.izzardink.com

Names: Archuleta, J. Reeder, author.
Title: The El Paso Red Flame gas station : and other stories / J. Reeder Archuleta.
Description: First edition. | Salt Lake City : Izzard Ink Publishing, [2022]
Identifiers: LCCN 2022019811 (print) | LCCN 2022019812 (ebook) |
ISBN 9781642280876 (hardback) | ISBN 9781642280869 (paperback) |
ISBN 9781642280883 (ebook) | ISBN 9781642280890 (audiobook)

Subjects: LCGFT: Short stories.
Classification: LCC PS3601.R389 E42 2022 (print) | LCC PS3601.R389 (ebook) | DDC 813/.6--dc23/eng/20220422
LC record available at https://lccn.loc.gov/2022019811
LC ebook record available at https://lccn.loc.gov/2022019812
Designed by Meighan Cavanaugh
Cover Design by Andrea Ho
First Edition

Contact the author at info@izzardink.com

Hardback ISBN: 978-1-64228-087-6
Paperback ISBN: 978-1-64228-086-9
eBook ISBN: 978-1-64228-088-3
Audiobook ISBN: 978-1-64228-089-0

Printed in the United States of America

TABLE OF CONTENTS

This one is for my parents, who came to stay.

JOLIE BLON

What remained of the afternoon sun balanced on the floor of the horizon and gusts of wind scattered the piles of brittle leaves at the base of the cottonwoods on top of the dirt berm. The leaves swirled in the cooling air above the small boy's head and then settled on the empty matchboxes he pushed around the small roads he had smoothed in the packed earth of the berm. He pushed the leaves out of the way but when they kept falling on his matchboxes he abandoned his imaginary highways and stood, brushing the dirt from his trousers. He could hear the steady drone of the tractor engine and turned to look over a small stand of salt cedars to the field on the other side. He could see Cecil on the faded red Farm-all pulling a brace of discs that cut long straight lines down the length of the field.

"Josh, come down here and clean up. Supper's ready," his mother called from the other side of the berm. There was a pot of stew hanging on a rod and bacon sizzled in the skillet at the edge of the fire.

"Okay, Mama," but he stood still and waited for Cecil.

Cecil brought the tractor up over the turn row to the bottom of the berm and cut the throttle, letting the engine idle. He then pulled a lever and lowered the brace of discs to the ground. Josh watched the cap on the exhaust pipe beat up and down in steady rhythm as Cecil kept the engine at a low idle, then he dropped the matchboxes and ran to the back of the tractor. Cecil climbed down, picked up the boy, holding him over his head, and sat him down on the tractor seat then climbed back up and stood on the axle next to the boy. "Do you remember where the throttle is?"

Josh scooted to the front edge of the seat and reached over to the right side of the steering column and pointed to the small red lever with a black knob.

"Okay, I want you to rev her a bit, but not too much."

Using both hands, Josh pulled the lever toward him and down and laughed as the engine speed increased and the exhaust cap bounced faster and then it stood straight up. Cecil let it run a while longer, listening to the boy laugh and then he reached over, pushed the throttle lever forward and up, turned the key and shut down the engine. It was quiet with the engine stopped and Josh could feel the heat from the exhaust and smell the gasoline and hot oil mixed with dust.

"C'mon, let's go eat," Cecil told the boy.

He picked Josh up and they got down off the tractor. Then he put the boy on his shoulders and carried him across the berm to the fire.

"Josh, wash up before you even come near the food!" His mother watched him as he went over to the basin and washed his hands and face. Cecil never washed before meals and Josh couldn't wait until he was grown up so he wouldn't have to wash before he ate.

They spooned stew onto their tin plates and sat around the fire and ate in silence. Josh's mother had been quiet all day and Cecil, sensing a storm, gave her plenty of room.

"Those are good biscuits, Belle." Cecil smiled at her.

She ignored him and sat close to the fire, smoking a cigarette. The brown cigarette paper was flat in the middle where there was not enough tobacco. Cecil liked to tease her about the way she rolled a smoke because she always spilled the tobacco and the paper always gapped open where she did not seal it properly.

Every payday he would buy a carton of Luckies but it had been weeks since Cecil had been paid and they had been rolling their own.

After a while Cecil said, "I believe that's the best rabbit stew I had in a while." He winked at Josh.

"Well hell that's the deal ain't it? You kill 'em and I cook'em." She threw her cigarette into the fire and went over to the washstand that Cecil had rigged on an old wooden crate. Josh was quiet because Belle was in one of her moods. He looked at Cecil out of the corner of his eye. Cecil smiled at him. Cecil had never gotten angry with Josh and always talked to him in a gentle way, especially when Belle was in one of her moods. He was a big man with an easy-going nature who liked to laugh a lot except when he drank whiskey and even then he just got real quiet. He usually only drank when he talked about someplace called Anzio. Josh thought that it must be a far-off place because it seemed like Cecil tried to find it when he drank and was quiet and the spark would go out of his eyes and he would stare out past the fields.

Cecil put his plate down and began to roll a cigarette. "What've I done now, Belle?"

"Nothin', just nothin'. How many times have I told you how tired I am of all this?" She waved at the tent and the car parked behind it.

"I told you, darlin', just another week and I'll finish the contract and we can move on."

She did not say anything and began picking up the plates. Josh felt his stomach shrink and he wasn't hungry anymore. Sometimes he heard them at night when they would argue in the tent. Belle wanted to settle down and she would question Cecil about what they were going to do when Josh was old enough to go to school. Belle wanted a house with wallpaper and a real bed and she wanted a decent stove and a sink and a lot of other things Josh could not remember. He had tried hard to imagine what it would be like to live in a house like that but could never picture it in his mind. He only knew moving from place to place and living in the tent and car except for the time they had lived for a short time in what Belle had called a "tourist cabin." He had good memories of that because it was warm and cozy and there was a radio and Belle kept turning the dial and would sing along with the music.

Cecil and Belle slept in the tent and Josh slept in Cecil's car on the front seat on a pallet Cecil made for him. He liked sleeping in Cecil's car. It was like having his own private tent. But sometimes in the middle of the night, his mother would come out of the tent and climb into the back seat of the car. She tried to be quiet but it always woke Josh. He would keep his eyes closed and pretend to be asleep but he would lie there awake and listen as she sobbed in the back. He did not know what to do when she cried like that and even though he knew he should do something he could never think of anything. One time he asked her what was wrong and she told him: "Oh, Josh just leave me alone and go back to sleep."

But he couldn't sleep. So he just lay there while she sobbed and then he felt tears sting his eyes and his arms and legs would get real stiff. He felt useless but he could not go to sleep until she stopped sobbing. He would wait for what seemed a long time and then when he heard her soft, steady breathing he would wait a while longer until he knew she wouldn't cry anymore and then the tightness would leave his body and he would drift off to sleep.

Josh looked into the fire and picked at the stew on his plate. Cecil smoked and watched Belle stack the dishes on the washstand. She banged the tin plates around and threw the knives and forks into the dish pan. Cecil rolled another cigarette.

"I think I'll go for a little stroll – c'mon Josh, you can go with me."

"He'll be stayin' here to help me clean up." Belle kept her back to Cecil.

"But Mama!"

"Hush up and get over here! You can dry while I wash." Josh watched Cecil get up slowly. Cecil winked at him and then walked down the edge of the field, disappearing from sight on the far side of the car. Josh was disappointed but he picked up the towel and went over to the wash stand. He liked walking in the evening with Cecil. It was always an adventure for him because Cecil could see ground squirrels long before Josh could spot them and he would laugh and point them out. And Cecil could see birds hidden in the trees and they would stop and watch until the birds sensed their presence and flew off. Once last summer they were walking alongside a ditch bank and suddenly Cecil grabbed Josh by the shoulder.

"Stay still!" He whispered. He cocked his head to listen and then Josh heard a sharp rattling sound.

"Don't Move!" And then "There he is!"

Cecil pointed to some weeds next to the water in the ditch. It was the first rattlesnake Josh had ever seen. They stood very still and quiet for what seemed like forever, then the snake, its tongue flickering, slowly uncoiled and crawled out of the weeds and slid across the ditch bank into the field. Josh felt his heart pounding in his chest. Cecil lifted his hand from Josh's shoulder and said: "Remember to always give a snake plenty of room and leave 'em a way out."

Josh remembered when Belle would walk with them. Belle and Cecil would walk real close together and talk and laugh the whole time. They walked so lightly on the ground it looked as if they were floating. Cecil would call her, "ma Jolie Blon", and Belle would smile and call him her "Bon Homme" and grab his hand and they would walk together holding hands. It had been a long time since Belle had walked with them in the evening.

In the morning Cecil went to work without breakfast. Josh ate biscuits and bacon and Belle drank coffee and smoked cigarettes. She sat looking into the fire, smoking and drinking coffee while Josh picked up the plates one at a time and took them over to the wash stand and dipped water out of the bucket into the basin.

In the distance they could hear the tractor as Cecil plowed the field that was on the far side of yesterday's field and after a while Belle got up and went into the tent. She came out carrying two suitcases and her coat and went over to the car and put them in the trunk.

"C'mon, Josh, let's go!" She was standing at the car.

"Where are we going, mama?"

"Just get over here and get in the car!"

He looked back at the fire and saw the rest of the bacon in the skillet begin to turn black and smoke.

"Mama! The bacon!"

"Josh, let's go and I mean right now!"

He hurried over to the car but he was not ready to go because he felt he had forgotten something. Belle lifted him up and put him in the back seat and went round and got behind the wheel. She started the car and in a moment they were heading down the dirt road that led out to the blacktop and the main highway. Belle never looked back.

Josh stood on the back seat and turned around to look out the back window. He could see Cecil's tractor in the distance, a small thing followed by a large brown cloud and in his mind he could hear the exhaust cap popping up and down. And then he remembered his matchboxes. He had forgotten them on the ditch bank!

"Mama! My matchboxes! I left them!"

"Oh Josh, I'll get you some more."

But Cecil had given him those matchboxes and Josh had watched as he had drawn wheels and doors on them and windshields and people inside behind the windows. Tears came to his eyes but he would not cry because Belle would just scold him. They drove on past old farmhouses and barns and Josh saw a tractor plowing a field near the road and it was then he knew for certain they would not ever be going back for Cecil.

After a while Belle started humming and then she began singing. She had a high, clear voice and knew a hundred songs and her singing always made Josh happy. He stood on the back seat with his arms across the top of the seat. The windows were down and the cool air blew into the back, drying his tears and carrying his mother's singing and after a while, the air and the steady hum of the wheels on the highway made him sleepy. He lay down on the seat and was soon sound asleep.

When he woke they were parked in front of a bus station in a town.

"Josh! Wait here – I'll be right back."

Belle opened the trunk, took the two suitcases out and closed the lid. Josh watched her walk into the station carrying the suitcases.

Evening shadows stretched across the front of the bus station and men in suits and women wearing dresses and carrying purses walked by the car and smiled in at him. In a little while Belle came back to the car without the suitcases. She got in, started the car and pulled out onto the main street of town. She was quiet as she drove and she leaned forward looking at the street signs. She turned down a side street and pulled into a lot with cars lined up in rows with numbers painted in bright colors on the windshields.

Belle got out and began talking to a large man who was wearing a tie and a straw hat. They talked for a while and Josh looked out the back window at the cars and a clothesline strung with yellow and red flags running from a pole at the front of the lot to a small building in back.

"I assume there is a clear title, ma'am?"

"Yes, it's in the glove box."

"And what are you looking to get for it, ma'am?"

"I know it's worth two-fifty."

The man frowned and Josh watched him as he walked around the car, examining it closely. He saw Josh standing on the rear seat.

"Howdy young feller!" The man had a double chin and kind, blue eyes.

"Well I could go one-seventy five. The tires are pretty bad and this paint is real tired."

"Goddammit! You know it's worth at least two-twenty five!" Belle was following the man around the car.

The man stopped, stepped back from Belle and took off his hat.

"It might be to you, ma'am, but I can't go higher than one seventy five."

Belle stepped closer to the man. "You wouldn't be trying to take advantage of a widow, would you?" Belle started for the driver's door.

"Ma'am, I am truly sorry for your plight and I would never take advantage, but if I agreed to more than one seventy five my boss would fire me and I need this job!"

Belle had the door open and stood there for a moment as if deep in thought.

"Well, if that's the best you can do."

"Yes, ma'am, that is the best I can do!"

"Well, ok, but I need to get some cash up front to take care of some bills today."

"Yes, ma'am, I can do that but I'll need to see the title."

Belle reached into the glove box and brought out an envelope with the title and handed it to the man. The man studied the title.

"Cecil Deveraux," He looked up from the paper, "Your husband?"

"Yes." Tears were in her eyes. "The war." She said. "Ma'am, I am so sorry for your loss."

"Thank you." She looked at Josh and then asked, "Will it take long?" She sniffled. "I mean, I need some cash now to repay a loan this afternoon ..."

"No, ma'am, it won't take long. I can give you some cash now and the rest when we have the papers drawn up and signed."

The man walked back to the office with the keys and the title. Inside the office the owner of the lot watched his salesman approach with the keys and title to Cecil's car.

"What's the deal?" He asked.

"She wants to sell it. There's a clear, signed title." The salesman handed the title to the owner.

"What did you offer?"

"One seventy five."

"You thinkin' what I'm thinkin'?"

The salesman shrugged. He did not like to think that the woman was dishonest and besides the little boy reminded him of one of his own. "She wanted some cash up front," he told the owner. Suddenly he did not like his job as much as he did at breakfast.

The owner grinned, "I guaran-damn-tee you that Mr. Cecil Deveraux is not dead and at this moment does not have a clue that his wife, or whoever she is, is selling his car. And once we give her some cash we'll never see her again. Oh, we may see Mr. Deveraux when he comes looking for his car but by that time the storage fees will add up to more than what the car is worth. You did real good, Wilbur." He went over to the desk and took out a small metal cash box. He removed five ten dollar bills and one five.

"This is a little bonus for you," he handed the salesman the five dollar bill. "And give her this," handing him the five ten dollar bills, "Then drive the car around back and park it way in the back of the shop behind those two big trucks. Not a bad deal for fifty bucks." He was smiling.

The salesman had a sour feeling in the pit of his stomach as he put the five dollar bill in his pocket.

When the salesman went back to the office with the title, Belle opened the door to Cecil's car.

"Josh, c'mon, get out of the car!"

"But mama, what loan—"

"Hush, Josh – just keep quiet until we get out of here!"

The man came back and counted out five ten dollar bills and handed them to Belle. He gave Josh three orange lollipops.

"Will a couple of hours be enough time?" She asked.

"Things may not be ready 'til mornin', ma'am. I need to draw up the bill of sale and check the title with the State boys and they're closed for the day."

Belle grabbed the man's hand with both of hers. "I hope you'll forgive my behavior and language…"

"Not at all, ma'am, it must be very hard, what with the little one and all."

Josh put two of the suckers in his pocket and was trying to unwrap the other when Belle grabbed his hand and led him toward the street. She held Josh's hand tightly and they walked quickly down the side street to the main street and turned left toward the bus station. At the corner Josh turned around and could see the man watching them from the lot. They walked down the main street to the bus station. Then they walked past it and went around the block to the back of the station and entered through the back door. Still holding Josh's hand Belle walked up to the ticket counter.

They stood in line while the ticket agent waited on a man ahead of her. She stood, quietly tapping her foot until her turn came.

"Yes, ma'am. What can I do for you?"

"Is there a bus to Dallas?"

"No, ma'am. You'll have to catch the bus to Odessa and then catch the Dallas bus from there. Would you like me to book you through to Dallas?"

"No, I have some kinfolk I can visit in Odessa and I'll just buy a ticket to Dallas after I'm through visiting."

"Yes, ma'am. The bus for Odessa leaves in thirty minutes. Just you and the boy?"

"Yes. Thank you." She handed him two ten dollar bills and he gave her back the tickets and her change.

They went over to a row of lockers and Belle pulled a round key out of her purse and opened one of the lockers. She removed the suitcases and carried them over to one of the portals where they sat on a long wooden bench to wait for the bus.

Josh was caught up in the noise and excitement of the small bus station with people coming and going and the announcer calling out the cities and the times for arrivals and departures and in a short while they moved over to the line of passengers and boarded the bus. Belle let Josh sit in the window seat and he tried to look out but could just barely see over the edge of the window.

He could see other buses and the tops of buildings and signs with bright colored lights that mixed together in bright streaks in the dusk. After a while they were clear of the town, out on the highway in the dark and Josh could look up and see stars in the clear sky.

"Mama? Who are we going to visit in Odessa?"

"Oh Josh!" She put her arm around him and pulled him to her and stroked his hair. "Whatever am I going to do with you?"

She held him close and began to hum softly and Josh felt safe and warm with his head against her chest, feeling the vibrations of her humming in his ear. After a while Belle stopped humming and he waited, his head rising and falling on her chest with each breath.

He was very sleepy but he waited until he could feel her breathing become soft and steady. He waited a bit longer to make sure she was asleep and would not cry. It was quiet in the bus and the soft whisperings of conversation drifted back to him as he thought about his matchboxes back at the ditch and Cecil on the tractor and about Belle and him riding down the highway in the dark and he wondered where they would be in the morning.

LA TORMENTA

The wind started somewhere north of the Oklahoma line and blew southwest across the Texas panhandle and then east over the peaks and valleys of the Mescalero Apache where it seeped into the passes of the Sacramento mountains and funneled directly south. It picked up speed south of the Sacramentos and was blowing at full strength as it moved over Crow Flat where it gathered up dust from the flats so that when it entered the valley it was no longer an invisible force. It flanked the valley, running to the east over the Salt flats to the Guadalupes, gathering sand before it hit the mountains. The mountains absorbed the storm's impact and pushed it south where it gathered more sand and dust adding a sting to its force, masking the granite rise of the mountains from the valley floor.

As it cut into the center of the valley, spreading west, it gathered strength and form rolling over the newly plowed fields, picking up dirt and dry pieces of cotton stalks and hulls which became the sharp edge of its force as it neared the town. The first windbreak of cottonwoods and cypress trees slowed it for a moment but after reforming south of the break, it blew with a new intensity, shrieking at the delay.

Its main force, blowing out of the north, mixed with the eastern flank and began to gain control of the valley.

It covered other windbreaks around farms in the north and howled through open barns and work-sheds, trapping equipment out in the yards. Irrigation pipes and empty oil drums were pushed around the equipment yards and out into the fields. Tumbleweeds bounced and rolled across dry fields until they became tangled and trapped along the fence lines and as the wind blew south toward the town, it gathered more dirt from the fields and pushed it higher until it formed a great dark rolling cloud, gaining speed and dimming daylight. With each new field gained and with the surrender of each farm, it reached higher, and blocked the valley floor from the sun's light. The sun gained small victories as its light shafted down through cracks in the storm's momentum, but in a while the sun's resistance was broken, the storm stealing more and more of its strength until, when it could be seen at all, it was only a small, dull orange disc. As it neared town, the storm added sound to its assault beginning with a gentle hiss, pushing dirt and debris, sweeping over the black top of the north road. As it entered the town the hiss took on a sharper tone, lifting the dirt and hurling it through the streets. The wind crashed into buildings, moaning down the sides, shrieking past cracks in windows and doors, seeking entry, changing rhythm, moving dirt and finding new targets.

The green cocktail glass and cotton bale painted on the front window of the Cotton Club Saloon were faded and worn away by years of wind and sun. The green lettering that named the saloon was splintered, melting into a memory of the prosperous years.

Josh sat on a stool at the end of the bar, his schoolwork spread before him. His books and papers lay on the bar top that was soaked through with years of spilled beer, scarred by smokes left on the bar edge or dropped from ashtrays, ignored or forgotten by men who were drunk or seriously engaged in conversation. The boy watched the fine dust sift through the gap under the front door and form soft brown drifts that would be blown level and spread deeper into the saloon with each strong gust, covering the gray concrete all the way to the shuffleboard in the middle of the room.

Three ranch hands were arguing at the other end of the bar, their hats moved up and down when they agreed and side to side on a point of contention. Two more played shuffleboard for a quarter a game, quietly concentrating on their shots, the only sounds from their game were the clicks of the pucks as they hit each other or a thump as they slid off the board into the trough.

The sheepherders watched the game from a booth in the corner, coins on the table as they bet on their favorite. They talked quietly over wine in their strange sounding language.

In the field next to the Cotton Club cars and trucks were parked at different angles. They were scattered about the field, each facing different points of the compass so that none blocked another's route home at closing time.

T.C. drove into the lot and parked his truck nose to nose against Willard's beat up old Chevy flatbed. T.C. switched off his lights, killed the engine and looked at Willard's truck. The wind pushed dirt up and over both trucks and occasionally a small tumbleweed slammed into their sides and slid up the fenders and over the hoods. He paid no attention to the wind. He pulled a cigarette out of its pack without looking at it, continuing to stare absentmindedly over the steering wheel and through the storm at the front of Willard's flatbed. He pulled a lighter out of the watch pocket of his jeans, brought it up to the cigarette, thumbed the wheel of the lighter and as he pulled the smoke into his throat her face stood out in the light of the flame. Her thick blond hair was pulled back and up and away from her ears, pinned at her neck and spilled down over the scalloped edges of a lace collar. Her eyes, full of mischief, teased him through the smoke.

He looked at her faint smile and thought that the photographer snapped the portrait too soon because a split second later he would have caught the open beauty of her full smile. But still, it was his favorite photo of her and he had mounted it on the dashboard years ago, before they married. He loved her more than anything or anyone in his life and he could hardly wait to be home with her tonight. He sighed and turned his gaze over to the back door of the bar. He meant to have a quick beer and talk with Willard about bringing this thing to an end once and for all, then he would hurry home where she would be waiting up for him, anxious to put this whole affair behind them. T.C. got out of his truck, held his hat firmly on his head and jogged over to the back door of the saloon.

The boy looked up from his books as T.C. entered the bar and several of the ranch hands looked up and greeted him. Willard sat on a stool looking into the mirror behind the bar and watched T.C. with a frown. The cowboys at the shuffleboard stopped playing and watched T.C. walk over to the bar and stand next to Willard. The men at the bar hushed their conversation. The click of dominoes at Rip's table and the sheepherder's quiet conversation were the only sound that could be heard over the wind.

"Willard, let me buy you a beer!" T.C. put his hand on Willard's back.

"Now, by God that's a great idea!" Willard shook T.C.'s hand. Conversation in the bar started again and the boys resumed their shuffleboard game with a disappointed but definite sense of relief.

"Claude, give Willard another Pearl and give me a GP!" T.C. instructed the bartender.

"No, Claude, let me have a Coors instead – since T.C. is buying." The bartender set the beers on the bar and Willard held his bottle up, studying it a moment.

"Thank you, T.C.!" He put the bottle to his mouth, turned it up and drained it in five or six gulping swallows. He placed the empty bottle on the bar and belched out loud. Josh giggled and Willard, smiling at the boy, let out another long, drawn out belch. He held the empty bottle up to T.C.

"Again?" He asked.

"Yeah, sure." T.C. signaled to the bartender who opened another bottle and set it in front of Willard. Willard immediately put it to his lips and drank half of it without setting it down.

T.C. and Willard spoke in low voices for a few minutes, then T.C. ordered a couple more beers and they moved over to a table away from everyone else. The boy went back to his studies and the shuffleboard and domino games went on.

The foreman of the sheepherders got up and went behind the bar for another jug of wine. The bartender nodded to the foreman. He kept the wine on the floor at the end of the bar near the sheepherder's favorite booth. The bartender never worried about it being so close to the patrons and on the fringe of his control since no one in town drank wine except the herders and, different as they were, they had yet to drink more than they could pay for.

The front door opened wide and Sean entered with the wind at his back, making the dust sing over the floor.

"Close that damn door!" Rip hollered from the domino table.

Sean closed the door, stood in front of it and announced, "God bless all here!" and then walked over to the bar and stood next to the boy.

"And what are we studying, Josh?" He asked, his huge hand on the boy's shoulder.

"History and math." Josh held his back straight against the weight of Sean's hand. Sean lifted his hand from Josh's shoulder and waved at the bartender.

"Harry Mitchell's, if you please, Claude, and a pack of peanuts!"

"I was a fair hand with the numbers m'self - - - and what is this history here?" He picked up the book.

"Texas History." Josh watched as Sean grabbed the bottle of beer the bartender had put in front of him. Only the neck of the bottle was visible in his hand as he put it to his mouth.

"Does it tell about the Irish at the Alamo in there?" Sean poured peanuts into the boy's hand.

"We haven't got to that part yet." Josh put the peanuts in his mouth one at a time.

"There weren't no Irish at the Alamo!" Clarence, the Catskinner, who was sitting on the other side of Sean objected. "They was Texans and other Americans but no Irish! The only foreigners there was the Mexicans and their general with a girl's name, Anna something or the other." Clarence spoke with authority.

"It was Santa Ana and there were Irish..." Sean was interrupted by a loud hiccup from Josh. He turned away from Clarence to the boy. Josh hiccupped again. He was embarrassed and tried holding his breath but succeeded only in smothering the hiccups as they kept emptying out of him.

"Hold your breath!" Clarence instructed. "You need to get control of your diagram!" Clarence spoke to Josh as a Doctor would a patient. Sean laughed so loud that he startled Josh.

"Control his what?" Sean confronted Clarence.

"His diagram! It's out of whack!" Clarence was indignant at Sean's questioning.

"You mean his diaphragm?' Sean was still laughing.

Clarence slid off his barstool and glared up at Sean, his head even with the third button of Sean's shirt. He spoke in a low voice.

"I reckon I know a thing or two about diaphragms and you don't need to be talking about those things in front of the boy!"

Josh sat there for a moment, waiting, amazed that just as quickly as they had come on, the hiccups had left him.

"See - - I told you!" Clarence pointed proudly at the boy.

Sean shook his head, knowing full well that he was at the losing end of this encounter with Clarence. "Right you are, Clarence. A fine bit of doctorin' if I say so m'self! Now, what'll you have?"

"Pearl." Clarence looked at Sean with suspicious eyes. Sean signaled the bartender for two more beers.

"Goddamit, Willard, you stay away from her!" T.C.'s voice was loud and desperate and it drew everyone's attention to his table. He pushed his chair back, sending it crashing into the domino players.

"Now, T.C., you got to tend to your homework and keep her home!" Willard stayed seated at the table and spoke to T.C. in a calm voice. T.C. stood there, his fists clenched.

"Besides," Willard continued, "You know damn good and well that I'm not the only..." T.C. leaned over the table and hit Willard in the face knocking his hat off and before Willard could respond, T.C. hit him again, opening a cut on his cheek. Willard jumped up and grabbed T.C. by the front of his shirt.

"You little bastard!" I can't believe you'd start a fight over that little bitch!"

Willard threw T.C. to the floor, jumped on him and began beating him with his fists. But T.C. squirmed and twisted under Willard's weight, making himself a hard target to hit,

Willard landed several solid blows, his fists making crunching sounds as they connected with T.C.'s face. T.C. finally managed to squirm out from under Willard and nimbly regained his feet. He was quick and before Willard could get his feet planted under him, T.C. delivered a leftright combination that staggered the bigger man.

The bartender ran to the far end of the bar and flipped a switch on the wall. Outside, at the top of a thirty-foot telephone pole, a red light blinked high above the building. It served as a signal to the deputy that there was trouble in the saloon. The light, which normally could be seen from the main street in town, blinked dully, its warning bleached to a dull pink by the blowing dust.

T.C. and Willard stood several feet apart, breathing in deep gasps, glaring at each other. Willard moved first and rushed T.C., grabbed him around the middle, lifted him off his feet and slammed him into the shuffleboard table. T.C. went limp and slid to the floor with Willard on top slamming fists into his face.

Sean and several ranch hands grabbed Willard and pulled him away from T.C. Willard's eyes were crazy and he was screaming. "I'll kill the little bastard!"

He struggled in the grip of the men who held him, his strength surprising them. T.C. rolled over very slowly and pushed himself off the floor. He stood, swaying a bit, studying Willard whose arms were pinned by the cowboys. Willard leaned back into the cowboys and kicked out at T.C. with both feet in the air at the same time. T.C. held both his hands up, palms out in front of him.

"Okay, Willard! I had enough, let's quit now!' His voice was quiet, pleading as he stood there, blood running down his face in lazy little streams. Willard continued to struggle, the cowboys held him tighter. Sean came over to T.C.

"Those cuts'll be needing attention."

"I'm Okay, Sean, I'll be going home now." T.C. continued to look at Willard, cocking his head to one side, the blood dripping from his face, splattering in tiny drops into the dust on the floor. He reached into his pocket and pulled out a set of keys. Then he walked over to the table and picked his hat up off the floor.

"I'm going now." He said.

Willard continued to struggle in the grip of the cowboys. He was in such a rage that he couldn't speak and growling, rasping sounds came up from deep in his chest. T.C. kept his eyes on Willard and moved toward the back door then he stopped and put his keys back into his pocket. He moved slowly toward Willard and when he got within several feet, he pulled a large Buck knife from his pocket and in one swift movement, opened it and plunged it into Willard's stomach. He stood there a moment and looked at the knife in a calm, detached manner, as if making sure that the knife went where he wanted it to go, then turned and walked calmly to the back door. Willard, who was still in the strong grip of the cowboys, stopped struggling and stared down at the black handle of T.C.'s knife. It stuck out of his big belly like a giant tick.

Everyone's eyes were on the knife and in the complete silence of the bar T.C. slipped out the door, leaving it wide open and in a moment they heard his truck start and then above the wind, they heard the sound of tires spinning in the gravel.

The cowboys released their hold on Willard and they all looked down at the knife planted in his belly. Willard grabbed it with both hands, holding it gently as he backed up to a chair and sat down.

He looked up at the faces in the bar as they continued to stare at his belly. He had a quizzical look on his face as if he was searching for answers to some question that he could not quite form. The bartender broke the silence.

"Josh, run down to the Lone Star and tell them to find Etienne!" Like most people in town, the bartender pronounced the deputy's name "Eight Ten."

The boy slid down from the bar stool and was out the front door in an instant. One of the sheepherders followed him to the door and closed it behind him. The bartender knew the Deputy could not see the red light in the storm and hoped he would be having coffee at the café.

Willard continued to stare at the knife and after a few minutes he stood up and quickly pulled it out of his body. A gasp went up from the men and almost as soon as it was issued, sheepish looks replaced the shocked stares and they began to move about and speak. A ranch hand noticed that the back door was still open and went over to close it. Others helped Willard to a chair. He held the knife in both hands, staring at it in wonderment. Sean gently took the knife from Willard's hand and placed it on a table. "Sure and Etienne'll be wantin' that." Sean pronounced the name correctly.

The bartender brought several clean bar towels over and placed them against Willard's belly. Rip limped out the door and in a few minutes he returned with a pistol stuck in his belt. The men looked at him, questions on their faces.

"The Deputy will be needin' help findin' T.C. tonight and I ain't goin' unarmed!" He announced.

Several of the men looked around the room, slipped out the back door and reentered the bar with a variety of revolvers and pistols. One carried an old thirty ought six. Willard sat in a chair and watched them

"Will somebody drive me home? I need to get some sleep!" Willard stood up, his face was turning gray.

"Sit down, Willard!" The bartender said.

The front door opened and the Deputy came in followed by Josh. He came straight to the back of the room where everyone was gathered around Willard

"How bad is it?' He asked Willard.

"Not bad, I don't think it got through the lard." Willard said. The deputy reached out very slowly.

"I'm going to take a look at it, Willard. I just need to open your shirt." He grabbed Willard's shirt with both hands and popped the snaps. The bloody material came away from Willard's hairy belly, exposing a small puckered slit that pushed out a small amount of blood, slowly but steadily. The Deputy leaned back and looked up at the men.

"It was T.C.?" He asked. They all answered that it was. "I need two of you to drive Willard into El Paso and four or five to come with me out to T.C.'s place. Did everybody see it?" Again everyone answered affirmatively.

"I don't need a doctor! I just need to get some sleep. I'll go into town and see a doctor tomorrow!" Willard's face was getting grayer by the minute. The Deputy stared down at Willard.

"Now, Willard, I'd like to explain all about blood poisonin' and shock and the like, but I ain't got the goddam time! You will get your ass to the hospital now or I'll place you under arrest and have you sent in handcuffs!"

Willard mumbled something under his breath as two of the men volunteered to drive him to El Paso.

"Raise your right hand!" The Deputy instructed. The two volunteers stood to attention, took off their hats and raised their right hands.

"You don't need your hats off to, oh hell! I hereby deputize you both! Now get him into El Paso as fast as you can. Do you know how to get to Thomason General?"

The volunteers said they did and with their hats firmly back on their heads they helped Willard out the door and into a pickup truck.

"Claude, I need to use your place here to run the manhunt. I want a central place for everyone involved in this to meet and stay in contact! Okay? Oh, and one more thing, anyone helping me on this, well, no more beer until it's over!" "I'll set up the coffee urn," the bartender offered. "Josh, run over to the café and get Sue Ann to send over a dozen sandwiches and a can of coffee!"

"Thanks, Claude. Rip, you, Sam, Johnny and J.T. want to follow me out to T.C.'s place?" The Deputy looked at their guns and the determined look on their faces. They nodded, not saying a word.

"Okay, you are hereby deputized!"

The Deputy then walked over to the sheepherders who were all standing against the bar with their foreman.

"Echeverria, I would like you and your boys to help out! Okay?"

"You bet, Etienne!"

"I need you to get over and wake the barber, tell him what's going on and use his telephone to call Sierra Blanca. Tell the Sheriff what happened and tell him that I'm going out to T.C.'s place looking for him. I don't expect I'll find him out there but maybe his wife will have an idea where he is. Tell the Sheriff I think he may be headed for Mexico. He has a fish camp down at Boquillas. Tell him to alert the Rangers, DPS, Border Patrol. The State boys can dig up the plate numbers for all his vehicles." The Deputy turned his attention to the herders.

"I want you boys to spread out and look around town and the valley and see if you can spot his pickup. I doubt he's in town but right now old T.C. ain't thinking, so who knows.

If you spot him, come back here. I'll be back directly. Do you all understand?"

The sheepherders had watched the Deputy with intensity as he gave his instructions. They all nodded at him and then asked him something in their strange language. The deputy answered somewhat slowly as if he had not spoken in that language for a long time and the men looked more at ease.

The Deputy turned to the foreman. "If you see him, don't try anything, just come back here and tell Sean what you found. I'll see you all back here in a bit." He turned and walked over to the bartender and Sean. The Deputy and Sean towered over the bartender.

"Sean, I would like for you to stay here and keep track of all the information that comes in on this." He reached over and grabbed the boy's school tablet.

"Write down anything you think is important and I'll check in with you when I get back. Claude, I want you to wrap that knife in a clean bar towel and keep it safe behind the bar. Rip, you and the boys come over here!"

"At T.C.'s house, Sammy and Johnny will go with me to the front door. Rip, you and J.T. set up at the back door but not too close. Stay back where you can see if anybody comes out but not close enough to get in the way. I've never known T.C. to be violent until tonight, so I don't know what to expect. But for God's sake, shooting him is the last thing I want. Do you all understand me?" The men all nodded.

"And you all treat his wife kindly. I don't need her getting any more upset than she probably already is. Remember his problem was with Willard." The Deputy paused, a look of surprise on his face.

"Sweet Jesus!! I forgot about Pete Jensen!! Wasn't him and T.C.'s wife..."

Rip interrupted him.

"Pete's been in Houston for over a week. But hell, Etienne!" "If we was to try to find everybody she ever - - well you know what I mean."

The Deputy took off his hat and wiped the inside hatband with a handkerchief.

"We best be goin'! You all ready?"

The small posse moved toward the back door. The bartender watched them leave and then went over to the coffee urn and checked the color of the water in the glass tubes. Sean walked behind the bar and grabbed a coffee mug from the rack over the sink. He opened a drawer and pulled out a tea bag.

"Still some left, I see!" He said.

"Ain't nobody drinks that stuff but you!" The bartender, lifted the lid on the urn.

"Won't be long 'fore the coffee's ready."

Sean opened the hot water tap on the urn and filled his mug.

An hour later the storm began to weaken, the steady assault breaking down into sporadic gusts, hurling dust and sand in diminishing blows. The interval between gusts was longer but the dying gasps of wind could still command the attention of those in the bar, warning them that even near the end this storm still had strength.

Sean sat at the bar, sipping tea and staring off into space. The fact that he appeared deep in thought disturbed the bartender who liked open conversation and was suspicious about too much reflection on any given subject.

"What the hell you thinkin' about?" He was wiping the bar with a clean towel.

Sean looked at him a moment before he spoke.

"I was thinking about Helen of Troy."

"Who's she?"

"My history teacher said that she was the prettiest woman in Greece!" Josh, whose presence had been ignored, spoke up.

The bartender, who was now threatened on two fronts, told the boy:

"It's time you went to bed. Gather your stuff and git! We'll clean the bar in the morning!" The boy gathered up his books. He was not sleepy, and wanted to stay and be part of the excitement.

"But what if you need me to run errands?"

"We'll handle things fine without you, thanks just the same." The bartender was firm. The boy slid down off the barstool, picked up his books and walked to the long hallway at the back of the bar that led past the bathrooms to a small storeroom and his cot.

"'Night, Josh!" Sean said.

"'Night, Sean!" Josh walked slowly, turning back to look at Sean and the bartender, hoping he would change his mind at the last moment. The bartender stood with both hands on the bar and watched the boy.

"Don't forget to wash up!" he instructed.

Sean continued to look down the hallway after Josh.

"Ye'll be earnin' points in heaven for takin' him in." he told the bartender.

"Humph!" I'd rather be earnin' rent for that cot!" The bartender began stacking boxes of empty cans and bottles behind the bar. He hated to admit it but he was curious about this Helen woman.

"Now. Who was this gal and what does she have to do with tonight?" He kept his back to Sean, trying not to show too much interest.

"Well, now, Helen's beauty was the cause of a lot of trouble for many a man, but I was only thinking of her in a symbolic sense. I mean, there were plenty of other beautiful women throughout history that caused at least as much grief."

The bartender felt trapped. This subject was beyond his understanding and with this Irishman you never knew where the conversation might lead. So he did what he always did when the subject was foreign to him. He tried to bring it back under his control.

"So! You're thinking that T.C.'s wife is causing problems cause she's beautiful?"

"Oh, she's a beauty! A prettier woman, I've never seen!" Sean said.

"Yeah! She's a looker all right!" The bartender agreed, his confidence restored.

"What I was thinkin' was that it's really not her fault but more like T.C.'s," Sean said.

"The hell you mean? T.C.'s fault?" a touch of outrage in his question.

"So I was thinkin'. It would be best for T.C. to let her go. She's a free spirit, that one. And free spirits can't be tied down. And marriage is…," he searched for a word, "restrictive to a free spirit. She can't be tied down to T.C. or any other man for all that."

The bartender came over and stood in front of Sean, both hands on the bar.

"You don't see, do you? He was fighting for his honor!

Everyone knew she was having a fling with Willard. Well, Willard and others too! But T.C. couldn't let anybody think he would let them get away with it!"

"I'll agree with you that's the reason he came in here tonight but what he was really fightin' for was something he wants to own. That's about possession! Don't ya see, Claude, he stabbed a man over what he was thinking is his property!"

"Well of course he did!" The bartender felt the advantage now, convinced that the Irishman was missing the whole point.

"She belongs to him! She is his wife!" He shook his head. He heard the back door swing open and the Deputy came in quickly followed by Rip and Sammy.

"Has Echeverria come back?" the Deputy asked the bartender.

"Not yet. Where are the others?" The bartender looked at Rip and Sammy. Rip was calm, Sammy was pale and looked like he was about to be sick.

"They're out at T.C.'s with his wife. Look, I got to get over to the Barber's and call the Sheriff. I'm not so sure now that T.C. is in town." The Deputy turned to Sammy. "Sammy, thanks for your help, why don't you take the rest of the night off. I'll see you tomorrow." He turned to the bartender and Sean.

"When Sue Ann brings the food over, give it to Rip. He'll take it out to the boys. Oh, and some coffee too. We'll be set up at T.C.'s all night. I'll fill you in later." He shook Sammy's hand and turned and went out the back door.

Sammy and Rip sat at the bar. The bartender brought them each a cup of coffee. Rip began sipping at his coffee but Sammy sat quietly, paler now with sweat forming on his forehead. Rip looked at Sammy's face for a moment then got down off his stool and went outside. He came back in a moment with a bottle of whiskey and put it on the bar. The bartender quickly reached over and laid the bottle on its side.

"Dammit, Rip, you know the law!" he admonished.

Rip gave him a look that asked for help. He shifted his eyes toward Sammy without moving his head. The bartender grabbed another mug, poured some whiskey into it, and put the bottle on a shelf under the bar. Sammy grabbed the mug and drained the whiskey in one gulp. The bartender opened a beer and set it in front of Sammy.

"What happened?" He asked Rip.

Rip lit a cigarette and took another sip of coffee before speaking. Sammy stared off into space.

"When we got out to T.C.'s we noticed right off that his truck wasn't there but lights was on in the house. So Etienne sent me and JT. to the back like we planned and he knocked on the front door. There was no answer, so he kept knockin'. After a while he yelled out to me and J.T. that he was goin' in. We kept watchin' the back and after a few minutes Etienne comes out the back door and signals for us to come in. Well, when we go through the back door, we could see T.C.'s wife sitting in a chair in front of a pot belly stove all wrapped up in blankets."

"Give me that bottle!" It was Sammy. Some of the color had returned to his face. The bartender poured more whiskey into Sammy's cup. Sammy drank it quickly.

"Is she alive or dead?" The bartender asked. He had reached a conclusion and wanted to be first to state it.

"Just how much of my whiskey are you plannin' on drinking?" Rip asked Sammy.

"Alive or dead?" The bartender repeated.

"Oh, she was dead all right!" Rip said. He took a deep drag on his cigarette.

"When I first saw her, I saw her from the back. There was still a fire going in the stove and her hair, you 'member her real pretty blond hair? Well, it was brushed real shiny and hangin'" down the back over the blanket. For a minute I thought she was alive." Rip flicked ashes from his cigarette into an ashtray.

"So! He went home and killed her, did he?" Sean was shaking his head in sorrow. "Such a pity!" Then, "God rest her soul!" He made the sign of the cross.

"He'll be facing the 'lectric chair now!" The bartender poured more whiskey into Sammy's cup.

Rip looked over at the cup and then into Sammy's face as he gulped down the whiskey. "Why the hell don't you just drink the whole damn bottle?"

Sammy turned to him, his eyes were bright and shiny, tears formed and began to run out of the corners. "I might need to." His voice was brittle.

Rip shrugged his shoulders. "It's okay, Sammy, it's all yours."

"So how did he do it?" The bartender asked, reminding everyone that he was the first to recognize the murder.

"Don't know!" Rip said.

"How d'ya mean?" The bartender bored in.

"Well, I told you she was wrapped in blankets from her feet to her neck. Etienne didn't want to touch anything until the Sheriff and the Coroner came over, so we don't know how she was killed." He sipped at his coffee and lit another cigarette.

"What I didn't know," he continued, "Is that when I first saw her after we came in the back door was that she was wearing a blond wig. It was the same color as her real hair, but it was a wig. I couldn't figure it out 'til I went around to the front of the chair."

Sammy let out a sob and drank more whiskey.

"All I could see was her head 'cause she was wrapped up in a blanket like I said but I could tell by looking at her she had been dead for a while 'cause most of the flesh was comin' off and she wasn't so pretty anymore. I figure she been dead probably ten days, coupla weeks. "

The bartender took his hands from the bar and stood back. "Jesus! You mean - - - !!?

Sean kept shaking his head. "A pity!" He said quietly.

They sat in silence, each lost in their own thoughts. The bartender filled a thermos and poured more coffee into Rip's mug. They looked up as Echeverria and his sheepherders came into the bar and went to their table in the corner. Everyone noticed that the wind did not follow them into the bar. The bartender went over and set a fresh jug of wine on their table. Echeverria came over to the bar.

"We find T.C. Two of the boys are out there with him.

"And where might he be?' Sean asked.

"Out north near the State line, just off the main road." Echeverria spoke quietly.

"Was he —?" The bartender began.

"Oh, he was very dead," Echeverria looked up with sad eyes. "He shot himself. In the head. There's not much left of…" Echeverria broke off.

Rip grabbed the bartender's thermos, "I'd best get out there and stay with him. Tell Etienne where I'm at." "Such a pity." Sean said.

There was silence in the saloon after Rip closed the back door and the men, avoiding each other's eyes, stared into the middle distance, remembering what they had seen this night and trying very hard to make sense of it all.

"Where's Sue Ann with those sandwiches?" The bartender asked no one in particular. No one answered so the bartender said nothing more. No one seemed concerned about the sandwiches. The sheepherders sipped their wine and any small sound in the bar echoed in the silence.

The wind came now only in small gusts and after a while it came not at all.

OLD DAN'S LAMENT

The dust devil slipped around the corner of the Cotton Club Saloon and blew dirt and bits of dry tumbleweed into Josh's face. He instinctively hunched his shoulders and closed his eyes tight shut. After tormenting him a few more seconds the devil spun across the street in front of the saloon and began to pick up speed over a plowed cotton field on its way to the school building four blocks away. Josh had been waiting for Rip O'Leary and Rip was late as usual. Rip operated on his own schedule and would arrive when it suited him. There were those in town who claimed that Rip was not dependable and that he talked far too much when he drank but Josh was too young to be much concerned about timeliness and schedules and he appreciated how Rip spent time talking with him and telling him stories. Rip and old Dan were among the few who never asked Josh questions about his life or where he came from. They accepted him just as he was and he felt as if they were kin. It was the closest thing to family that he had in a long time and so he never passed up a chance to ride along with Rip to deliver supplies to old Dan.

The dust devil spun across the cotton field and lifted a thin cloud of dirt, spreading it out as it rose higher. At its base, where it was thinnest, another spray of dust spread out like spikes at the bottom of a yucca. Josh watched the dust devil move quickly over the field and across the dirt road bordering the football field. When it hit the football field, which was in flood irrigation, the dust devil broke up and as it spun out it faded into a light ghost of brown before it finally disappeared.

The sound of Rip's pickup truck turning off of Main Street brought him out of his thoughts and he turned to watch as the truck came to a rattling stop in front of the saloon.

"Ready?" Rip asked.

"I am!" Josh opened the door, jumped up on the running board and looked into the bed of the truck. There were six cardboard boxes pushed up close to the cab and all were filled with canned goods and bottles.

Rip revved the engine and ground the gearshift lever into low gear. They turned right at the hardware store onto Main Street and Rip ground through the gears as they drove north out of town.

"Need to adjust that clutch!" Rip offered as an excuse. He held a bottle of beer and gripped the steering wheel with the thumb and remaining two fingers of his left hand. He shifted gears with and held a cigarette in his right hand. They drove north past the picture show and the high school.

Josh looked at the schoolhouse as they drove past. The grass was being watered and it looked cool under the shade of the cottonwoods in front of the building.

"You gonna be in high school this year?"

"Yep."

"You signed up for the team?"

"I did."

"Here!" Rip pulled a bottle of soda from a bucket half filled with ice resting on the seat between them. Josh could see one more bottle of soft drink among the bottles of beer in the bucket. He took the soda, liking the cold wetness of the bottle in his hand.

"The church key is in the glove box." Rip pointed.

Josh reached into the glove box and retrieved the bottle opener and carefully removed the bottle cap. He drank slowly taking small sips trying to make it last all the way out to old Dan's.

"When's the last time you seen old Dan?" Rip asked.

"Couple of months ago when they brought some ewes and lambs down. He went back that same day, so I only saw him for a minute."

"Yeah. I tried to get him to stay and get drunk, but he wouldn't. Said he had to get back."

Josh sipped his drink and thought about Dan and the sheep and about how people talked about him. They drove on in silence and in a while they were at the end of the paved road. The truck rattled and creaked as they left the pavement and rode over the washboard surface of the dirt road. Rip reached into the bucket and handed Josh a bottle of beer.

"You want to open this for me?"

Rip put the empty bottle on the floorboard.

"You want the empties?"

"Thanks." Each bottle brought him two pennies at the Cotton Club.

Just after they crossed the cattle guard at the state line Rip stopped the truck.

"Gotta take a leak!" He waited for the road dust to settle and then climbed out and limped to the back of the truck.

"There's a sandwich and a couple of apples in a sack in that big box if you're hungry."

Josh had not eaten all day so he opened the door, stood on the running board and took a paper sack out of the box. Rip got back into the truck and ground his way up to third gear.

Josh put the unopened sack on the seat between them. His stomach growled and his mouth watered as he thought about the sandwich. He waited for Rip but he was lost in thought, sipping his beer and smoking as he drove. Rip finally noticed the unopened sack.

"Well? Ain't you hungry? Go 'head and chow down."

Josh's hand shook as he opened the sack. He unwrapped the waxed paper and held the sandwich up to Rip who shook his head.

"I ain't hungry. You go 'head and eat, I'll get something later at old Dan's."

Josh took small bites and chewed slowly fighting his desire to gulp the sandwich. He stopped several times and put the sandwich down to open bottles of beer for Rip. The food in his stomach and the heat and movement of the truck over the rough road made him drowsy. He kept himself awake by looking out for pronghorns as they drove north over the creo-sote covered flats.

Rip sipped the beer, and flicked his cigarette out the win-dow. He reached into his shirt pocket pulled out another, lit it and remembered the first time he laid eyes on Josh.

It was a Saturday night when Josh and a woman named Belle came into the Cotton Club. She never said it but everyone assumed that Belle was Josh's mother. Rip had never met Belle before but he had known many like her. He always enjoyed talking with her and flirting more than a little and he would have liked to get to know her better but she loved to dance and with his old wounds he just could not keep up. Besides she was attracted to men with more money than Rip had or ever would have.

Then one day he found Josh sitting on the bench in front of the Cotton Club. He remembered the boy sitting there, his back stiff as a board, holding tightly onto a small battered grip and staring intently at the mountains east of town.

"Howdy, Josh, where's Belle?"

"She had to go see some kin in East Texas but she'll be back real soon." Rip remembered that the boy did not look at him while he spoke but kept his eyes fixed on the mountains. That had been six years ago and Belle never did come back and after that day Josh never mentioned her again.

The boy never complained and never asked for anything ex-cept work so he could earn his own way. Rip had convinced old man McCormick at the Emporium to hire Josh to help unload the trucks that brought supplies from El Paso once a week. At first the old man was reluctant but he kept an eye on Josh, who without being told would sweep out the old warehouse, stack cans, wash windows and would not stop working until he was told to. He gladly hired him for the once a week job. Rip had also talked Bobby at the Red Flame into letting Josh do odd jobs at the gas station after school and on weekends.

"Hell, I don't even know if she was his real mama." Rip drained his beer, put the bottle on the floor of the truck and grabbed a full one from the bucket. He frowned and seemed to struggle with a thought then his face relaxed and he sighed as if he had come to a decision.

"Ever wonder 'bout old Dan's face?" Rip's voice startled him from sleep.

"Huh?" Josh opened his eyes.

"I said, ever wonder how old Dan's face got that way?" He handed Josh the bottle for him to open.

"I heard he got like that in Korea."

"That's right."

"Were you there, Rip?"

"I was." Rip turned and looked at the boy. "You wanna hear the real story?"

"I do."

"Okay. I'll tell you the story but I don't want you tellin' it to nobody else." "I won't."

" 'Cause nobody but family and friends need to know.

Got that?"

"I do."

Rip reached into his shirt pocket, got another cigarette, put it in his mouth and lit it with his Zippo. His eyes were fixed straight ahead through the windshield.

"Dan and me grew up together right here in this valley. We went to high school together and played football together. We even dated the same girl. Well -- I mean at different times of course. The war ended the same month we started the ninth grade. I dreamed of joining up and getting in on the fighting but by the time I was old enough they were sending all the boys home. So there we were. Two kids out of school, full of beans and rarin' to go! Dan had taken up with Betty Jane Morley. That was the gal I said we both dated. Well, actually, I dated her first but it didn't last long 'cause she always kinda had her eye on Dan. Anyway, they started dating when they were in the tenth grade. I never held any hard feelings over her choosing Dan instead of me. I knew right off we wasn't right for each other. She liked readin' and poetry and stuff like that and all I wanted was - - well, anyway, now this might surprise you but old Dan, he always liked to read even back then. Betty Jane always said she wanted to be a teacher and I'll be damned if old Dan didn't tell me one day when we was fixin' flats down at the Humble station, that he was thinking about goin' off to college and being a teacher too."

"Now I knew he was smart and all but I couldn't picture him being inside, wearing a tie, working for some four-eyed old principal or maybe even a woman? I needed to have a serious talk with old Dan."

"Bout that time Betty Jane started goin' to some Woman's teacher college over in east Texas and Dan, he was gettin' serious 'bout goin' to some college over there, too.

"Like I said, we was both workin' at the Humble station then. The valley was boomin'. Cattle and cotton was king and there was jobs to be had everywhere. One day old man Mather comes into the station and I'm out there filling up his truck and checking the oil and he says to me as I'm washing his windshield: "You don't know a couple of fellows looking for some hard work and good pay, do you?"

"I told him I sure did. I was kinda tired of pumpin' gas and fixin' flats so I went in and talked with Dan and convinced him that we could work the ranch a year or so, he could save his money and then go on over to east Texas to college. He was pretty stubborn against it but I told him that old man Mather wanted two hands and if Dan didn't sign on with me I might not get on neither. Well, old Dan finally agreed and that's how we come to be cowboyin' up in New Mexico."

"Dan and Betty Jane wrote to each other all the time. Every evenin' he would write her a letter. I never could see what he was writing but I bet it was poems or somethin' like that 'cause he'd be writing along in that old shack where we bunked and then he'd stop and look up at the ceiling like he was thinkin' real hard and then he'd go back to writin'."

"He even saved up enough money to take the train to Dallas and see her. That summer when he got back from visitin' Betty Jane, he told me they was plannin' a wedding and would I be his best man?"

"Well 'bout that time the US of A was havin' some trouble with the communists in Korea and before you know it there was fightin' and the U.S. was in it. Well hell! I was kinda tired of cowboyin' and I saw this as a chance to do what I missed out on in dubya dubya two. I was talking about it with the foremen who was in the war and he told me that if I was going to get in on the action to join the Marines. He said you could be guaranteed a fight if you was in the Marines, where if you joined the Army or Navy you might end up fixin' flats or peelin' potatoes. That old codger said he'd go back in a minute but the Japs shot him up pretty good in the war and the Marines wouldn't let him back in and he said he'd be damned if he would go hat in hand to any other outfit."

"I was tellin' all this to Dan but he was thinkin' 'bout marrying Betty Jane and this was takin' up most of the space in his head. So I started in talking 'bout how he could use the GI Bill to get him through college just like the World War Two vets was doin'. Besides, I told him he didn't have enough money to get married."

"Old Dan was not good about savin' money. Not that I was either, but he spent it in different ways. Like for example when we would go to El Paso with a load of cattle or to pick up supplies, I'd slip over to Juarez for Tequila Sours and a quick trip to Boy's Town. Old Dan would stay in El Paso and spend his money on books. Books!"

"So on the way back to the ranch Old Dan would be haulin' a bag of books and I'd be haulin' a hangover and some real pleasant memories. But that's what I mean 'bout savin' money. Neither one of us had much saved so the money part and the GI Bill made sense to Dan."

Josh finished his soda and put the bottle on the floor with the empty beer bottles. He opened another beer for Rip as they began the slow climb from the flats up into the hills.

"They sent us to boot camp out in California and…"

"What's boot camp?'

"Basic training." Rip looked at Josh. "Where they teach you how to be a Marine."

"And after that they put us on a big troopship. We all stood at the railings and sang as we watched the lights of San Diego getting' smaller as we sailed away." "What song did you sing?" Josh asked.

"Well, Josh," Rip was patient. "We sang '*Goodnight Irene*' and it was kinda sad to be leaving. Dan called it a melancholy moment and it was going to get more melancholy for me 'cause I got seasick after we stopped singing and stayed that way damn near the whole way across the ocean. We finally got to Korea and was sent up north." Rip paused. "Well, I started out to tell you about old Dan's face but here I am ramblin'on." Rip was quiet for a minute or two. "What happened before is stories for another time, maybe when you're older. But I wanted you to know about Dan and how he got that way and up on that hill was where it happened. We were dug in along the ridge and I was in a hole near to another hill. Dan was over to my left nearest the machine gunner. It was winter in Korea and I was never so cold in my whole life and the Commies just kept chargin' up the hill at us day and night, blowin' their damn bugles. They wore white and it was hard to see them in the snow, 'specially at night.

"But we looked for shadows when our flares would go up 'cause they would lay down and be real still. Whenever we would see a shadow we'd aim to the side of it and that's how we got a lot of them. Anyway they kept chargin' and shootin' and throwin' grenades and we kept shootin' them down. There were so many of them we just had to pick our target and shoot, jam another clip of ammo into our garands and shoot some more. I didn't see it but some of our boys on the left flank of our lines was overrun and the Chinks shot them up and bayoneted them somethin' awful. We lit into those bastards pretty good and after we run them off the hill the Lieutenant got a few of us together and we carried the wounded about 25 yards behind our holes where the corpsmen worked on them."

"What's a corpsman?" Josh asked.

"He's a medic. A swabbie who…"

"What's a swabbie?"

Rip sighed loudly. "Look, Josh, there's goin' to be a whole lot you ain't gonna understand but how 'bout holdin' all your questions 'til the end, else I'll never finish."

"Where was I? Oh yeah – the Lieutenant was hit in the face by a ricochet and he just reached over and pulled the bullet out and went on about his business. He was a tough old boy from Texas and had been on Iwo Jima. It made you feel real good that somebody like him was in charge. Them damn Commies kept on comin', blowing their bugles and tryin' their best to kick us off that hill but we kept pushin' them back down the hill."

"There was a couple of Marines down the slope who were shot up pretty bad and I saw Dan and a Sergeant movin' down to drag them back up the hill. The Sarge was hit and went down and didn't move and then Dan was hit but he kept crawling toward them wounded Marines. He grabbed one of them by his parka hood and started dragging him back up the hill. We were firin' like hell trying to give him cover. The Chinks were throwin' grenades at Dan and he went down again but he got up and kept draggin' that Marine. I jumped out of my hole and run down to help Dan."

"When I got to old Dan he was gruntin' and breathin' real hard. I grabbed another wounded Marine and started back up the hill. A couple of the other fellas come down and our machine gunner was goin' crazy, hollerin' and firin' to beat the band. You could see the tracers and hear the rounds snappin' by and I was sure hopin' he was killin' a bunch of them bastards. We got the wounded back to our position and the Lieutenant, who looked real bad with blood froze all over his face, was tellin' us to move the wounded to the rear. We put them on blankets and drug them back to the corpsmen when a grenade went off and the Lieutenant went down. Dan started over to the Lieutenant but he was hit and he went down too. Grenades was comin' in real heavy. They were what we called 'potato mashers' and you could always see them because of their smokin' fuses."

"I grabbed one and threw it back down the hill but another one went off near Dan's head. When I got to him I thought he was dead, 'cause his face was real chewed up and I could see a lot of bone and blood so I grabbed him and dragged him to the rear. That's when I felt somethin' hit me in the leg and knock me flat on my ass."

"There wasn't any pain but I was real upset that they had got me. A corpsman came up and grabbed Dan and took his ammo pouches and handed them to me. So I crawled back up to the holes to see what I could do. That's when I got hit in the hand – blew the fingers clean off. I could still shoot but was havin' trouble reloadin' so I pushed myself over to the machine gunner and started helping him out with my good hand. He told me I looked like hell but he was glad to see me anyway and then I don't remember anything until I woke up in a tent at the aid station at the bottom of the hill."

"There was a guy who was on the rack next to me and he was gruntin' and cussin' tryin' to pull on his boots. I asked him what he was doin' and he said he had to get back up the hill to his squad. He finally got his boots on and was limping toward the tent flap when a corpsman comes over and gives him hell for gettin' out of the rack." This guy tells the corpsman to go to hell and the last I saw him he was leavin' the tent. I know how he felt 'cause I wanted to be back up there with the boys instead of layin' around on my ass, so I thought, hell, if he can do it so can I. I saw they had put a big bandage on my hand and I couldn't feel my leg so I tried to roll over and get to my feet when a corpsman comes runnin' over cussin' to beat the band."

"I heard him yellin' somethin' about a bunch of idiots and then I passed out. When I came to I knew my fightin' days was over for a while. I asked the corpsman about Dan and he pointed to a rack where Dan was layin' with his head all covered in bandages. "

"I was havin' trouble stayin'awake but I remember they loaded us into some trucks and we ended up in a place called Hungnam where they put us on a ship and after a while we ended up in a hospital back in California."

Rip was quiet for a while and Josh sensed that he wouldn't put up with any more questions so the miles passed in silence. Finally Rip said: "They called it a 'police action' but it was war pure and simple! Me and Dan talked about it a lot and we don't agree on a lot of things but we both think that up there on that hill – well, – it was the finest thing we ever done." Rip's eyes were bright and he was lost in thought for several miles. He sipped beer and slowly smoked a cigarette looking out the windshield at someplace very far away.

"Betty Jane came to California and visited Dan at the hospital every day. She told him she would drop out of school and finish it later so she could be with him after he got out of the hospital. And that's when old Dan started to change. He would be downright mean and ornery to her. I had already been discharged so I would spend time with Betty Jane and Dan at the hospital and her eyes would be all puffy and red from cryin'. She said Dan told her he didn't want her around and that he wasn't goin' to marry her. Now you gotta remember that his face was pretty awful, much worse than it is now. The doctors made it better but they never could get it bent back to the point where it was easy to look at him. But that didn't seem to bother Betty Jane none. She said that Dan was a 'beautiful man'. I never heard anyone, not even a woman, call a man beautiful but she did. She said she didn't only love him for his looks but she loved him for who he was." Rip drove in silence for a while, a frown on his face.

"I mean, me and Dan was close as kin and it was all I could do to look at his face without wanting to turn away. I did finally get used to it but it sure took a long time. Dan told the doctors that he didn't want Betty Jane to visit him anymore, that she was causin' him upset and the like. Well, the doctors talked with Betty Jane and she hung around for a while but after a week or so she went back home. She told me before she left that Dan's mind was weary from the war and all the pain and that he would return to bein' his old self and would get around to askin' her to come visit. She said she would just wait 'til then."

"She wrote him every day. I know 'cause everyday there would be another letter on the table next to his bed. He asked me to throw them out but I just took and kept them in a box. I wouldn't a felt right throwin' them out. He never opened a one of them. I must have had 'bout fifty or so letters when they finally stopped comin'."

"Later on that year Dan got out of the hospital and he come home. He stayed with his folks out at the farm and never did go out. I was the only one, other than his folks, that he would visit with. After a while, he started actin' a little like his old self and we even got drunk a couple of times, but he mostly kept to himself and his books."

"A couple of months after Dan got back, old man Mather sent word to me that he would like to hire me and Dan back on. I drove out to Dan's place and told him about what the old man said and I'll be damned if old Dan didn't jump at the offer. Me? Hell, I couldn't sit a horse anymore and I was gettin' along fine with my disability check. Besides I didn't really feel like bustin' my ass for nobody anymore."

"So I drove old Dan up to the Mather ranch and the old man asked Dan if he would like to stay out at the east mesa place and run that part of the operation. I hadn't seen Dan so happy since before we left for the Marines. The job was no heavy liftin' and I think old man Mather knew Dan wanted to be away from people. Anyway that's where old Dan's been ever since and except for you and me bringin' him things from town once a month, it's just him and his dog and his books." Rip chuckled.

"Achilles. Why the hell would you give a dog a name like that?"

"Did Betty Jane ever come back?" Josh asked.

"Nope. Her and Dan was quits for good. She married a teacher fella and they're both teachin' in El Paso. I saw her last year at the homecomin' and when she asked about Dan I saw that old look slip into her eyes but after a while it slipped right back out."

"After seein' her like that I thought it might be a good idea to take her letters up to old Dan. If he wanted to throw them away – well he could just do it. Like I said, I wouldn't a felt right throwin' them away. So I took them up with the supplies that month. Dan never said a word, just put them on the table with the other boxes and never mentioned them to me since."

The sun cut through the rear window of the truck and glittered over the dust on the dashboard. When they neared the base of the mesa the white clouds that hung over the mountains began to darken and push higher, forming large grey puffs that flattened at the top. Rip studied the clouds with a frown.

As they began the climb up the mountain they would roll up the windows to shut out the road dust as it swept over them in the corners of the switchbacks. They would roll them back down as the truck picked up speed on the straights and the dry, hot air flowed through the cab, drying their sweat. They climbed higher and Josh could look out over the flats to the mountains to the south. The horizon was clear, the sky a milky blue but he knew Rip was worried that clouds in the east would bring rain to the mountains and turn some of the arroyos they had to cross into rivers. He had seen only one flash flood but had been frightened by the fury of the water as it roared down the arroyo under a bright blue sky.

In a while they reached the top of the mountain. It was table top flat for miles and he could see Dan's place at the base of some small hills in the north. The wood of the buildings was a weathered ash grey and stood out against the scrub oak and cedar of the hills.

The happiness he felt every time he saw the place lifted his spirits and he couldn't wait to see old Dan and Achilles. He loved exploring the hills with Achilles, wandering for hours, the dog running ahead flushing out jackrabbits and quail from the cedar. When Achilles was younger he flushed several porcupines and got a snout full of quills and it took old Dan all afternoon to remove them. Dan lit into Josh about taking better care of Achilles and about how he should be more responsible with animals in his care.

On the occasion of their visits Dan would fix a pot of stew or chili and they would eat their fill. Later, as Rip sat on the porch drinking whiskey, Dan would tell Josh stories, sometimes reading from the many books in the shack. Dan always called it "holding school" and Josh enjoyed the stories even though he was almost always sleepy after the big meal.

At the top of the mesa it was clear and hot but there was less dust and they enjoyed a clear, easy run over the last few miles. They saw Dan's horses in the corral on the far side of the yard as they pulled into the open space in front of the shack. Rip leaned on the horn three times and then climbed down from the truck. Josh lifted a box of groceries out of the back of the truck and took it up to the house.

"Hey, Dan!" Rip shouted. He stopped on the small porch outside the front door. There was no answer.

"He's probably down feedin' the hogs. Bring the rest of the stuff up here and I'll go fetch him." Rip told Josh.

Rip limped across the field and Josh watched as he went out of sight behind the barn. Josh brought the other boxes to the porch and then sat down on the edge, his legs dangling, enjoying the thin breeze in the shade. He sat for a while then went over to the water tank under the windmill and splashed water on his face and head. He felt the drag on his fingers as he ran them through his hair which was full of dust that turned thick as it mixed with the water.

He closed his eyes and put his head underwater in the tank holding his breath as long as he could, then lifted his head and felt the cool trickle of the water running down his neck before it evaporated in the hot puffs of the wind, so dry it almost crackled. He stood there a while listening to the blades of the windmill creaking in the wind and then he went back to the shade of the porch but before he could sit down he saw Rip coming around the side of the barn. He had a frown on his face and his quick movements made his limp more pronounced. Josh stood, knowing something was not right.

"It's Dan!" Rip said. He came up onto the porch and opened the door and Josh followed him inside. Everything was as Josh remembered. The bed on one side of the room and the stove on the opposite side. The bed was made with military precision, two blankets folded neatly on the chest at the foot. There was another chest, open and full of books. There were several fruit crates overflowing with more books under the bed.

Rip grabbed the blankets and went back outside.

"Josh, I'm goin' to need your help."

"What's wrong?" Josh followed Rip out to the truck.

Rip stopped and faced Josh. "Dan's dead."

"What? How…?"

"Just c'mon, Josh!"

They climbed into the truck and Rip ground into low gear and drove around the barn past a pile of cedar posts and down a slight incline to the hog pens. Josh saw Dan as they came closer.

He was lying on his back next to the feed troughs, a bucket lay next to him on its side, hard feed was spilled around him. Achilles was standing next to Dan, his tail down as he watched them approach. He made low growling sounds as Rip and Josh walked toward him. The smell of the hog pens was strong in the heat and Josh noticed that there was not enough wind to keep the flies off Dan.

"Josh, I need you to get Achilles settled down. He likes you better'n me and he doesn't know what we're up to."

Josh called the dog's name softly and moved very slowly toward him. Achilles continued to growl but eventually stopped and began wagging his tail as Josh walked slowly and carefully around Dan. Josh knelt down and called softly to the dog. Achilles, his tail wagging, moved over to Josh and ignored Rip.

"It's okay, Achilles, you done your job real good. We'll help out now." Rip laid one of the blankets on the ground next to Dan.

Josh held Achilles and looked at Dan. Dan's right arm was flung out under the bottom rail of the fence next to the hog troughs. All four fingers were missing down to the second joint. Some of the bone stuck out past the flesh looking like small white knobs in the dirt and spilled feed.

Rip saw Josh staring at the hand.

"The hogs did that. They'll eat anything and when they couldn't get the feed - -well, old Achilles kept them from gettin' more of him." Rip stood and looked at Dan.

"I want you to take Achilles up to the house. Give him some water and put him inside. Then I want you to get four or five empty feed sacks out of the barn and come back down here."

Josh hurried up the hill to the house with Achilles wagging his tail at his side. Rip started the truck, turned it around and slowly backed up to Dan's body.

When Josh returned with the feed sacks Dan was laying face down on one of the blankets. Rip had let down the tailgate of the truck. He took the feed sacks from Josh, doubled each one over and laid them on the floor of the truck bed, He then placed a blanket over the sacks.

"Okay, Josh!" I need you to grab the blanket at Dan's feet and help me lift him into the truck."

Josh felt a little lightheaded. He grabbed the blanket and on Rip's command he lifted. As he lifted he heard a gurgling sound and smelled something he had never smelled before. He felt panicky then his stomach lurched.

"It can't hurt you Josh, so just ignore the smell! That's all it is. Just a smell."

Rip lifted his end of the blanket so that the upper part of Dan's body rested on the edge of the pickup bed.

"Hold on now!" Rip climbed into the bed and pulled Dan all the way up so that he lay next to the pallet of feed sacks.

"Okay, now we need to roll old Dan over on to his back on this pallet."

Josh grabbed Dan's boots as Rip took hold of his shoulders and they gently turned him over onto the blanket covering the feed sacks. Josh's head was still spinning and as Rip put up the tailgate and secured it with the chain, Josh leaned over and vomited. Rip stood at the back of the truck and watched as Josh vomited several more times. Josh straightened up and was embarrassed to see Rip watching him.

"It's okay, boy. It's natural and the best thing you can do." He patted Josh on the back.

"You never seen anybody dead before?"

Josh shook his head. He was afraid to speak as tears stung his eyes.

"I'm not saying you ever get used to it, but…" His voice trailed off and he went around to the front of the truck and took the water bag off the grill.

"Here! Drink some of this. It'll help settle your stomach and give you something to puke up if you need to again."

Josh rinsed his mouth, the water tasting sweet against the bile. He gulped down several swallows and then put the bag back on the front of the truck.

Rip had started the truck and was waiting for Josh to get in. Josh told him that he wanted to walk back up to the house and

Rip nodded without comment. Josh's legs were wobbly at first but by the time he reached the barn he felt better. Rip was standing on the porch when Josh came up to the house.

"We'd best load them groceries back up!" Rip pointed to the boxes on the porch as he went inside. Josh took the boxes one at a time and put them into the back of the truck. He tried not to look at Dan.

Rip brought a pillow out from the house and Josh watched as he gently lifted Dan's head, slipped the pillow under and very slowly, as if trying not to wake him, put his head back on the pillow. He then placed the other blanket over Dan tucking each side under his body. Rip knelt beside Dan, looking at his face for a little while then gently put the top of the blanket over Dan's face and tucked it in under his head on the pillow.

They packed all of Dan's books into another trunk and loaded them into the truck snug up against the cab. Achilles watched them and made soft whining noises while they worked.

"Okay now, I want you to feed the horses and hogs and make sure that there is plenty of water for them. I'll gather up the rest of old Dan's stuff. Hurry up 'cause I want to be off this mountain before the storm hits and the arroyos are runnin' full."

After feeding and watering the animals Josh came back up to the house. Rip had put more empty feed sacks in the bed of the truck and Achilles was laying on them next to Dan. He continued to make soft crying sounds, like a kitten mewing. He would get up and turn a circle or two then lie down and then get up and do it again.

"Let's get movin!" Rip limped around to the driver's side of the truck, looking up at the clouds. Josh climbed into the cab.

He noticed a small box on the seat and some clothing on a hanger covered in tissue paper, hanging behind the seat.

"His dress blues." Rip offered as an explanation. "We'll bury him in those and I don't want them gettin' all dusty in the back."

Josh put his hand on the box.

"Those are the letters I told you about." Rip removed the top of the box. Josh saw that each letter was neatly slit open along the top.

"I know the letters was still sealed when I brought them up here. I wonder when it was that he started into readin' 'em?" Rip shook his head.

Halfway across the mesa Rip stopped the truck.

"Josh, there's a bottle of Waterfill and Frazier in one of them boxes. Fetch it up here, will you?"

Josh found the bottle of whiskey and brought it up front to Rip who twisted off the top and put the bottle between his legs.

"He sure as hell never said a thing to me 'bout readin' the letters." Rip put the bottle to his lips.

"Is Dan with Jesus now?" Rip swallowed some whiskey.

"With Jesus?!" He looked at Josh, irritation plain on his face. He took another sip of whiskey. Josh continued to look at Rip his question hanging between them.

"I don't know, Josh. I suppose if he believed in God then - - -. Come to think of it I do believe his folks was churchgoers." Rip thought about it for a moment. "Well I hope he's with him then."

"Don't you believe in God, Rip?"

Rip made a snorting sound and kept quiet for a while. Then he answered in a quiet voice.

"If you're talkin' about faith in God I'm not sure I under-stand all I know about that. It's supposed to make you strong but on the other hand I seen some real weak folks with lots of faith so I'm not sure how that's supposed to work. It's a real fragile thing and I couldn't never hold onto anything like that for very long. To me it's more 'bout hope than faith and I never did give it much thought except over there in Korea after I got hit and was afraid of dyin'. It was the loneliest I ever been in my whole life. Like I was a three day ride from nowhere."

A question formed in Josh's mind but after looking at Rip's face he knew better than to ask it.

They began the drive back down the mountain and watched the dust blow in thin brown gusts, from east to west across the flats. The wind always came before the rain. The sun was still bright in the western sky and Rip was confident they could get through Arrowhead Canyon and be out on the flats before the rain.

Josh looked back into the bed of the truck and saw that the blanket had come loose at the top and dust was swirling around and settling on Dan's face. Josh stared at Dan's face. It had be-come a splotchy beige mask with the dust but it did not look as raw and mutilated as before. He felt his legs shake and all the energy drain out of him. His thoughts may as well have been out there in the wind on the flats, blowing around in the mes-quite and creosote. He was very tired and he wished he were somewhere else.

"The blanket's come undone," He told Rip.

Rip nodded and brought the truck to a slow stop. He got out and covered Dan's face with the blanket, taking his time in tucking it back under Dan's head. When he climbed back into the cab he saw that Josh was crying silently, staring out the front of the truck, the tears making muddy tracks in the dust on his face.

Rip started the truck and did not look at the boy as he ground through the gears. He lit a cigarette and smoked quietly as they drove across the flats. After a while he asked in a quiet, gentle way.

"Who you cryin' for, boy?" "What?" Josh wiped at his face.

"I said who you cryin' for? Old Dan back there or yourself?"

"I don't know."

"Well you'd best think on it 'cause it does make a difference!"

Rip continued to smoke as they made their way off the flats and into the hills in the north end of the valley. He slowed for the cattle guard at the State line and then picked up speed as they crossed over onto the black top. It was quiet as they drove on the paved road and with no trailing dust the speed of the truck blew away the layers of road dust. Rip looked over at Josh.

"They's two rules 'bout cryin', Josh." The smoke from his cigarette curved over the steering wheel and was sucked out the wing window.

"Rules?"

"Rule number one is: It's proper to cry over the dead and dyin'."

He was silent, waiting for the boy's question. It did not take long. Josh sniffled and looked at Rip.

"What's the second rule, Rip?"

"Don't never let anybody see you do it!"

They rode on in silence. Josh didn't think he had any more tears in him as he watched the town take shape in the distance.

Rip chuckled and shook his head.

"Now, how in hell am I goin' to get shed of all them damn books?"

HOMECOMING

The cottonwood trees that stood between the high school building and the football field still held onto most of their leaves but they had begun to take on that dry brittle appearance which along with the dormant Bermuda grass and a chilled breeze out of the north signaled the start of winter in west Texas.

On the field a crew of men were marking it for the homecoming game and there was yellow twine stretched tight between steel pegs which served as guides for the twowheeled hand cart that spread the lime in narrow lines on the dry Bermuda grass. For the last few home games the field would be hard as concrete.

Josh watched the crew as he stood under the goal posts in the north end zone. This would be his last homecoming game and he had decided that he would try his best to remember every moment of the occasion. He wore his blue letter jacket with his name embroidered above the school initials. The marking crew were all graduates of the high school and had played when the school had been a power house of six-man football. The old-timers referred to those times as the glory years and the marking crew wore the grey letter jackets from that era. Their jackets bore the patches that proclaimed District, Bi-District and Regional championships. These veterans of the glory years called the recent teams the "slick-sleeves" because since the school began playing eleven-man football they had not even won a District championship.

The end zones were open to the dirt roads that ran by the north and south ends of the field and the crew had marked a semi-circular double line ten yards beyond each end zone that served as a boundary for the spectators who drove their cars and pickup trucks to the game.

By game time this area would be filled with people from the valley, many wearing the grey jackets, drinking whiskey and visiting as they sat in or on their vehicles. They were true critics of the game and were not shy in their criticism of the coach and his team. Tonight's opponents, the Clint Lions, were an old rival from the 6-man years. Josh and his team had not beaten Clint in four years and the critics were not happy.

The sun was low in the west and the air was becoming more chilled. Josh watched the crew for a while longer then walked over to the Gymnasium and the dressing rooms.

The dressing room had recently been painted gray and the new paint made the walls look cold but it covered up the smell of dried sweat and old cement. He undressed and hung his clothes on a wall peg. The blue home jerseys and new white game pants were hanging inside the lockers and clean socks were on the floor next to each player's cleats.

He took his game jersey and began working it over the shoulder pads. The tightly woven cotton of the jersey was stiff and it was always a struggle to pull it over the pads. He preferred slipping the pads into the jersey and then pulling the whole thing over his head rather than putting on the pads and having a team mate tug and pull the jersey over his head and shoulders. After he finished with the shoulder pads he slipped the thigh pads into the new game pants, picked up the hip pads, thought about them and then put them back in the locker.

He pulled on his pants and felt the stiffness of the new fabric stretch as it settled on his thighs. He put on a t-shirt and then laced up his pants. He grabbed each kneepad, twisting them from side to side, making sure that they fit tightly. The kneepads were built into this new style of pants but Josh preferred the old pants that had pockets for the pads so you had a choice of wearing them or not. He pulled on two pair of socks so that his shoes would fit snug on his feet and decided not to have his ankles taped tonight because he thought it robbed of him of his flexibility and slowed him down.

He stuffed his cleats into his helmet, picked up his jersey and shoulder pads and walked, in his stocking feet, over to the training room to wait for the rest of the team.

He lay on his back on the floor, in front of the chalk board, his head on his jersey and shoulder pads and closed his eyes; the clean, sharp fragrance of the analgesic balm and astringent was strong in the room.

In a short while Bryan, James and Lorenzo came in. Bryan immediately went over to the chalk board and started drawing up plays. Lorenzo and James put their gear on the floor next to Josh and lay down flat on their backs.

"Heard 'bout the coach?" James asked.

"What 'bout the coach?" Josh kept his eyes closed. "The school board's looking to fire him." "What the hell?" Josh sat up.

"Some people on the board say he's a boozer." James said.

"Oh that's bullcrap!! I've never seen him take a drink! Have any of ya'll?" Bryan came over from the chalkboard.

"No, but they say he gets drunk most every night after he goes home."

"I got an uncle that drinks too much so I reckon I can tell a boozer when I see one and I say Coach is not a boozer." Lorenzo said. "'Sides, if he drinks at home it's nobody's business."

The door opened and a couple of other teammates came into the room.

"Danny, you're Dad's on the school board, what do you hear about them wantin' to fire Coach?" Bryan asked one of the new arrivals.

Danny opened his mouth but said nothing and he quickly looked away from Bryan. He moved over to the training table and kept his back to the group.

"Come on Danny, what do you know?" Bryan pressed him.

"'Sides, maybe he has a reason to drink!" Lorenzo was talking to the group. "He was shot up pretty good during the war and he also got some kinda fever from the jungle." "Danny??" Lorenzo would not let up.

"I heard the board thinks his drinking is a bad influence on the students." Danny turned around and held up his hands as if pleading with the group.

"How can he be a bad influence if nobody knows he drinks?" Josh asked.

The door opened and Mr. Smith, the assistant coach came into the room. The discussion ended abruptly and everyone in the room looked directly at Mr. Smith.

"Mr. Smith, are the rumors about the school board and Coach true?" Bryan asked.

Mr. Smith was the science teacher, a dry and fussy man.

"Now boys, all I can tell you is if the coach wanted you to know something he would tell you himself. He wouldn't appreciate you all guessing about and gossiping over rumors.

So I ..."

At that moment the Coach strode into the room with two trainers and other members of the team and he immediately began barking orders.

"Bryan, I want you and Lorenzo at the chalkboard! Josh and James help Mr. Smith get the playsheets handed out. Anybody that needs taping get over here on the table! And everybody finish suiting up, we got a lot of ground to cover!" He moved over to the chalkboard and immediately began discussing some of the newer plays with Bryan and Lorenzo, the co-captains.

The coach's demands and taskings in the pre-game meeting and the intensity of the preparation pushed all thoughts of the rumors about the school board and the coach out of the boys' minds and in a while the familiarity with the pre-game routine and the coach's confidence served to convince them in the end that the rumors were just that – rumors. Besides none of them wanted to think about a day when the coach wouldn't be there.

After they went over the plays for the last time and the signals for tonight's game were reviewed and when the last shoelace was tied they gathered around the coach in the middle of the room.

The coach's strong voice filled the room.

"This is our homecoming. A school tradition. But this night is about more than you and me and a football game! It is a Homecoming for your families and friends, your classmates and older men who sweated and bled on this field in years past and many others who have come great distances to be here on this special night. They would not be here if they did not believe in us and know in their hearts that we can beat this team. We've had a good season so far and we have given them hope."

"They, like me, have no doubt that we can beat this team! All these people know another tradition! A winning tradition! A tradition that this school is famous for!" He paused and looked around the room.

"We can beat this team but we can't slack off for one second." The coach's voice was steadily growing louder.

"I need one hundred percent from each of you for a full four quarters! For every play! Every down! For every second we are on the field!"

The adrenaline began to flow in Josh. He felt the energy of the team. Their minds were already on the field. They were restless, their feet moving, their cleats causing a muffled clattering on the rubber matting in the training room.

The coach was quiet a moment. He looked around at his team. "Will you give me that much tonight??" "YES!!" They roared.

"Okay, then..." he paused. "Now join me in the Lord's Prayer." The coach's strong voice led and they all joined in. "Our Father who art in heaven..." Josh closed his eyes and prayed as he had done before every game but his mind was on the field thinking about the plays and new signals for tonight. After the Lord's Prayer, they came out of the training room in pre-arranged team order. Coach, the co-captains and the first string led with the subs and trainers behind. They walked carefully on the cement apron outside the training room door, their cleats in a full clatter, slipping in their hurry to grind them into the earth and begin their run to the field.

The crowd roared as they ran onto the field. And as they formed ranks for calisthenics car horns blared and the sound of whistles and cowbells poured down from the stands. Josh's heart was so full he could barely catch his breath.

The butterflies began their flight somewhere between the Star Spangled Banner and the school fight song. He stood on the thirty-yard line and looked downfield at the other team, holding his helmet under his arm, hearing the pep squad sing about honor and loyalty and victory. His stomach was full of butterflies and they were trying to get out. He knew they would stay with him all the way down the field and would stop only when he hit his man or was hit himself.

The fight song ended and he put his helmet on. The other team had won the coin toss and chose to receive. The field was light straw in the fall evening, fresh lime marked the sidelines and crossed bright and clear every five yards between him and the other team. The breeze out of the north whistled through his helmet but soon became muffled by the growing beat of his pulse thudding in his ears.

His body tensed at the referee's whistle and he began his run when he saw the kicker's foot meet the ball. The yard lines flashed by under his feet. His eyes were on the two receivers as they waited for the ball. They were small but very fast and he knew that the best way to stop them was to hit them before they turned up field.

As he ran downfield the blockers faded back to the receivers, forming a screen. He quickly spotted the blocker who had been assigned to stop him. He picked him out of a group of three who formed their left flank to protect the runner's sideline path. His man locked eyes on him as he closed the distance. The receiver on Josh's side of the field caught the ball and ran to the opposite side. He saw that the screening blockers on his side did not move with the receiver and he slowed his pace, suspecting a reverse. His view was partially blocked but he could see the receiver on the far side move toward the ball carrier and Josh's side of the field and he knew at that moment where he would make his move.

The blockers began their screening move in his direction. His man was biggest of the three and was the outside flanker of the screen. Josh picked up speed, closing the distance and hit his man hard before he had a chance to plant both feet. He heard a sharp crack in his left ear as his shoulder pads slammed into the blocker's chest. He heard him grunt and smelled onions as the blocker's breath left him. The blocker was down. Josh recovered his balance and now had a clear shot at the ball carrier who was moving laterally toward his sideline. He knew he had to hit him quick before the runner made his turn and outran him up-field.

As he slowed his pace to protect the sideline path his peripheral vision picked up a blur on his left and he felt both disappointment and satisfaction as James caught the runner from the side and knocked him completely off his feet at Clint's twenty two yard line. He locked hands with James, helped him to his feet and saw the dazed look on the ball carrier's face turn to a grimace when he pushed himself up off the ground. The crowd cheered and James grinned as he heard them call out his name.

They formed a huddle and Earl called the defensive play. Clint had a powerful running game and always started their plays from scrimmage with a run off-tackle. They did not care that every team in the district knew this. This was their opening challenge every time, win or lose.

Josh lined up at right inside linebacker and began studying the backs and linemen. Clint went with a quick snap and ran their right halfback off right tackle. They gained five yards on the play and Josh noticed that the left offensive guard was slow in leaving the line to make his block. He watched closely during the following plays as the guard moved about a half step slower than his teammates. Clint continued their march downfield, three to five yards at a time. This was their strength. They would patiently grind down and wear out defenses with the run and only then mix in some passing plays.

Clint crossed midfield after another set of downs and Coach signaled to Earl that they had to penetrate into the backfield and stop Clint before the plays developed. Earl told Josh to rush the quarterback and he would stay home to cover the pass.

He and Earl planted themselves close behind the defensive line as the quarterback began to call the count. At the snap Josh dipped his right shoulder and rushed at the gap between the guard and the center. The guard tried to recover but he was too late and Josh was in the backfield. He reached the quarterback as he back pedaled on a pass play. He hit him hard under the left armpit and felt the quarterback's wind explode out of him as they hit the ground. He heard the crowd screaming but did not realize he had caused a fumble until Earl helped him up off the ground. James had recovered the fumble and the referee blew his whistle and signaled first down for the home team.

Bryan ran in from the sidelines and called them to the huddle.

"Let's go, let's go!" Bryan looked around the huddle. "Fake forty three, right buttonhook on two! Josh, give me ten yards before you hook in the flat. Break!"

Josh lined up at right end and on the snap he rushed straight downfield. The defensive end played off of him giving him lots of room. He stopped and button-hooked at ten yards. He had a moment of panic as the ball was almost on him when he turned. He felt the ball hit just above his belt and locked it home with both arms. He turned toward the sideline and just started to square his shoulders downfield when the defensive end hit him from behind and stood him up straight. Then the outside linebacker hit him hard from the side and drove him several yards forward.

He got up and handed the ball to the ref who was already signaling first down. Bryan called two running plays in a row and in a blur they were on the Clint twenty yard line with another first down. In the huddle Bryan called another pass.

"Josh, go ten to the post and then cut to the flat. Let's keep that outside linebacker in this time. Fake thirty three right flat pass on three!"

At the snap Josh angled straight at the post, ran past the outside linebacker who had been pulled in by the fake and then he broke for the sideline. Again the ball was almost waiting for him. It was out in front of him, chest high. He snagged it easily and brought it in before he ran out of bounds. Another first down. On the way back to the huddle Josh felt some satisfaction as he watched the chain gang move the chain downfield.

In the huddle Josh was winded and noticed that he had knocked the skin off the knuckles of his right hand.

Bryan called a fullback run up the middle and James went into the end zone standing up. The crowd went crazy. It was almost too easy and because it was too easy Josh was worried.

They scored again at the end of the first quarter and Clint answered with a field goal. They had been successful with short flat passes and buttonhooks throughout the first quarter and Clint was finally tightening up their defense in the short secondary.

At the beginning of the second quarter they held Clint to three first downs, stopping most of their running plays and had gotten to the quarterback three times on pass plays. He did not fumble again but the Clint quarterback was obviously rattled and they heard him voice his frustration to his offensive line.

On fourth down Clint punted from their own forty yard line and James ran it back to mid-field.

In the huddle Bryan called Josh's number on a post pattern.

"Josh, buttonhook at ten as usual and then break for the post. I'll hit you deep. We'll pull them in with a fake draw. Earl be sure you block that nose tackle. He 'bout ate my lunch twice! Forty one fake, deep post right on four!"

Josh got set at the line and watched the defensive end. Frustration showed on his face and he gave it away by clenching and unclenching his fists. Josh's confidence grew.

At the snap he ran straight at the defensive end who was playing him closer now. Josh stopped and hooked at 10 yards and when the end moved toward him he took one step toward the sideline and then turned and sprinted for the post. Out of the corner of his eye he saw the defensive end try to turn and go with him but it was too late. Josh had three or four steps on him and he knew that the end could never catch him now. As he cut toward the middle of the field he checked for the linebackers and was shocked to see that the outside back had not been taken in by the fake run and began turning to cut Josh's angle to the post.

Bryan already had the ball in the air. Josh was flying over the grass, his feet only touching the ground long enough to propel him faster down the field. The linebacker was positioned to cut him off and intercept. He kept running, his arms already out. He concentrated on the ball and tried to ignore the linebacker and stay completely focused.

The linebacker dropped out of his peripheral vision and he watched the ball, a perfect spiral, begin its downward arc. He no longer felt the ground. He was disconnected from the earth, moving to the spot where the ball was falling to the field. His arms were out, fingers stretched wide. If he could touch it he could catch it. He did not hear the wind, he did not feel the blood rush through his body. He only felt his flight across the field, the speed, a calm rush, eyes wide, the ball spiraling downward, the only thing of value in his world. If you can touch it you can catch it! He stretched his arms out further and felt the smooth grain on his fingertips, his eyes wide, his two hands pulling the ball to his chest. Only then did he look to the goal post. He was at the ten, the five and into the end zone. Where was the linebacker?

He heard the crowd explode. The pep squad was running down the sidelines waving their pom-poms and cheering. He slowed, stopped and turned back to the field. The referee had both arms straight up in the air, whistle in his mouth. Josh handed him the ball and began looking for the linebacker. Bryan and the team gathered round him and patted him on the back as they jogged back to the sidelines.

"What happened to the linebacker?" He asked.

"He slipped and fell when he tried to cut back to the post. Better lucky than good, right Josh?" Earl said.

"Yeah. I'll take it." Josh answered, grinning.

The coach called Josh and Earl over. "Earl, you and Josh stay here with me on the kick-off." Coach never relaxed during the game. He was always thinking several plays ahead.

"I want you to keep pressure on the quarterback! You got his attention! Let's keep it! I want you two to alternate rushing. Josh, you got the left guard figured out. Keep working on him! Keep the pressure on. It's only the second quarter!"

They went back on the field for Clint's first play from scrimmage. Earl rushed first and caught the fullback in the backfield.

On the next play the center moved over to cover for the guard and blocked Josh's rush at the line. The ref whistled the play over and as Josh was starting back to the defensive huddle, the left offensive guard shoved him from behind. He caught Josh by surprise and partially knocked the wind out of him. A knot of pain developed under his shoulder blade. The ref penalized Clint fifteen yards for unsportsmanlike conduct. "We got 'em rattled now!" Earl said.

"Oh, I'm real happy 'bout that." Josh was trying to get his breathing back to normal.

Josh and Earl lined up behind the defensive line and Josh could see the guard glaring at him. Josh grinned back at him. "Set, hut – hut!" The quarterback called cadence looking out at the defensive secondary. The ball was snapped and Josh again rushed the gap between center and guard. The quarterback kept the ball and ran to his left. The center, quicker than the guard, blocked Josh full on and stood him up straight. Josh tried to slide off the block to the outside with his eyes on the quarterback. He squared his shoulders to the line and had just turned his head when he saw a quick blur in front of his face. It felt like someone hit him in the face with a club and then he felt nothing.

When he came to he was on his back trying to suck wind into his lungs. Coach and the others were standing over him. He blinked his eyes, trying to focus. Everything was a blur. There was no pain but he had trouble breathing and something warm was bubbling out of his mouth and running down his chin and neck.

"Josh! Can you hear me? Can you see me?" Josh recognized Coach's voice but he was so far away!

Josh started to speak but his mouth was full of liquid and it was running down his throat and he began to choke. He wanted to tell the coach he was fine but couldn't get the words out.

"Josh, listen to me!" Coach's voice was calm. "Can you move your legs?"

Josh moved both legs.

"Good!" Can you move your arms?" Josh moved both arms.

"Good! Now listen to me. I want you to get up and walk with me off the field. Understand?" Coach was down on one knee, calm as ever.

Josh nodded and immediately knew he made a mistake. It felt like his teeth were trying to work their way out his head. Someone was trying to take his helmet off.

"No!" Coach quietly instructed. "Leave his helmet on!" Josh got to one knee.

"Keep your head up, Josh." He heard the coach's calm, clear instructions in an echo.

"Okay. Now I want you to get to both feet." The coach's voice was soft. "I'll be here, right here next to you,

Okay?"

Josh got to his feet. He started to touch his face with his hand.

The coach grabbed his hand. "No, Josh. Not yet." Earl, James and others were standing behind the coach. They were staring at his face and they all looked like they had just seen their best dog run over by a truck. He was concerned but still did not feel any real pain as long as he held his head still.

"I want you to walk with me back to the bench. Hold your head up! Don't let them rag-knots think that they hurt you!"

Coach's calm, quiet instructions steadied Josh. "The guard caught you with a forearm shiver. The center and him set it up."

They walked to the sideline. Josh saw his teammates and the crowd behind them. They were all clapping their hands and their mouths were open but all he could hear was the coach's voice over a dull roar in his head. His thoughts were all jumbled. His vision was beginning to clear up and he noticed the blood covering the front of his white game pants.

"Your nose is broke, Josh. In fact it's broke pretty good, but a broke nose ain't the end of the world. I ought to know." Coach's calm voice reassured Josh. "Now Doc Snead will take you to the dressing room and fix you up. I'll see you at halftime."

Josh walked with Doc to the dressing room and halfway across the field the numbness began to wear off and each step made Josh's head throb with pain.

Doc had him sit on the trainer's table and carefully removed his helmet. He gently held Josh's head, looking closely at his face. "You're probably wondering what the hell the County Vet knows about broken noses." He was looking at Josh's face from all angles. Josh smelled whiskey on Doc's breath. "Well, you would be right. I am more comfortable castratin' hogs, calving and treatin' horses but by God, if I do say so myself, I'm hell at settin' broken bones and noses."

"If it'll make you feel any better I'll have you know I've set a couple of dozen broken noses and never had a complaint." He had not touched Josh's face but was still examining it closely, talking quietly all the while. "Of course they probably don't complain because I don't charge for it but still and all…" Doc's voice faded and he was looking at Josh's face straight on as if he were taking measurements.

"Now to do this…" Doc's voice was detached as if he were talking to himself. "I'll have to take hold of your nose a bit— really is best to do this right after it's broken and still numb…"

Josh squeezed his eyes shut as Doc gently grabbed his nose.

"Now I want you to count backwards from five to one. Out loud. When you get to one I want you to yell it out Okay?" Doc's grip tightened on Josh's nose.

"Okay, Doc."

"Start counting!"

"Five, four…" Josh felt a sharp crunch in the middle of his face and his head filled with pain. He lost his breath and saw bright flashes of color flying through the space between him and Doc. He closed his eyes but the flashes were still there.

"There! Good as new! Well, almost."

He opened his eyes to see Doc, his head canted to one side, looking at Josh's face.

"I'm going to stuff some gauze up your nose and I want you to leave it there 'til Monday. I'll take it out then."

Doc went over to the sink and brought back a glass of water and three aspirins.

"I want you to take three aspirins every four hours but no more than twelve a day. Got that?"

"Doc?"

"Yes, Josh?"

"Do you ever let anybody get to one?"

Doc chuckled. "Take this towel, soak it in cold water and start cleaning up some of the blood."

They could hear the crowd cheering at the end of the first half and within a few minutes Coach led the team into the dressing room.

"Everybody get a coke and then on the floor at the chalkboard!" The coach headed straight for Josh.

"Nose looks good. How you doin'?"

"Okay, Coach." His own voice was strange to him. A muffled, stuffy voice.

"Good, now listen up. At the end of halftime I want you to put on your helmet and walk back out on the field with me." Josh looked at the coach, not understanding.

"I don't have time right now to explain but I want you to stand with me on the sideline and hold my clipboard. I want you to look at it, even if you can't see it and I'll talk to you about the plays. Nod your head when I talk to you and keep your eye on the game. Got it?"

"Got it!"

The trainer brought over a clean pair of game pants.

"Billy get one of those new face bars and screw it onto Josh's helmet."

Josh sat on the trainer's table and tried to concentrate on the coach's critique of the first half and his plans for the next two quarters. Billy brought him his helmet with a face bar attached. Josh held the helmet by the guard and fought off the first wave of nausea.

At the end of halftime Coach handed Josh his clipboard and they walked side by side out of the dressing room onto the field. Josh had trouble at first adjusting to the face bar. It was a new and strange presence in front of his face but he thought it would have come in handy in the second quarter.

They passed by the referees and the chain gang on the side-lines. The head ref came over and asked about Josh's nose. The coach kept walking to his side of the field and replied in a loud voice. "It's broke! He wants to go back in but I'm thinking I'll keep him out most of the second half!"

The ref gave the coach a knowing look. "Right." He said.

Josh stood next to the coach on the sidelines during the second half as the coach instructed. Several times he felt like he was going to pass out and the field and the players on it tilted in his vision.

The coach kept a close eye on him and when he felt Josh was close to his threshold he would tell him to take a knee.

Josh would gratefully go to one knee and try to keep his mind on the game. Halfway through the third quarter, the dizziness went away and by the beginning of the fourth quarter, with the exception of the throbbing in his nose, he began to feel better. He turned and looked through the crowd to see if Missy was there but could not find her. Once, as he was scanning the crowd he saw Roble. She looked at him in her direct manner. Her dark eyes looking right at him. She smiled and waved.

Josh was disappointed that he couldn't see Missy but quickly recovered as he watched the opposing team struggle on the field. Clint never recovered from their surprise in the second quarter and could not mount a good offense in all of the second half.

The game ended with the score twenty-one to ten and Josh forgot about the pain, joining in the celebration and accepting congratulations from his teammates and friends in the crowd. Cindy, one of the cheerleaders, ran over to him, gave him a hug and told him she would see him at the dance. He watched her run over to join the other cheerleaders who were on their way to midfield to meet with the Clint pep squad.

He watched the Clint team walk off the field. They were silent, their heads down, walking slowly, holding their helmets. He looked for the offensive guard and the center but could not make out the numbers on the jerseys as the team walked out of the light of the football field to their busses in the school parking lot.

As he began walking across the field to the dressing room Roble caught up with him. "Hi!" She said.

"Hi yourself!"

"Your nose doesn't look too good." She studied his face with her bright dark eyes.

"Well thank you, Roble. It doesn't feel too good either!"

"Your eyes will probably turn black tomorrow." She took his hand.

He stopped walking and looked down at her.

"Do you have anything good to say?"

"Well, you did catch a beautiful pass and win the game!"

"We could have won without it but thanks anyway."

She stopped walking and reached over and took hold of his helmet.

"Can I carry it off the field for you?" She looked directly into his eyes.

He chuckled at her audacity. It was tradition for a player's steady girlfriend or his parents to carry his helmet after the game. Josh had always carried his own. He held tightly to the helmet looking at her. She met his look without blinking. He relaxed his grip and she took it from him. She held onto his right hand with her left and swung the helmet at her right side as they walked off the field. "I'm spending the night at my tia's house and I'm going to the homecoming dance and I would really like to dance with you but you probably can't dance in that condition."

He was trying to think of a clever reply but his mind was still a bit muddled.

She let go of his hand and took longer strides so she could get in front of him and look at his face. "I saw you looking for someone in the stands. You weren't looking for me were you? I bet you were looking for Missy!"

"Roble!"

"Well she didn't come to the game. I came to see you play and she didn't!" Josh sighed.

"But I didn't like seeing you get hurt, Josh." She grabbed his hand and held it tight.

They walked in silence through the shadowed light between the field and the gymnasium. Her small hand was warm in his and he felt her firm grip. They walked past the bleachers and through the cottonwoods and he could have sworn that his nose did not hurt so much. He looked at Roble walking next to him and noticed her hair. It was soft and a violet black, shining in the half-light, bouncing as she walked.

The Community Center building was hot and crowded. Josh sat at the team table up on the bandstand and sipped at a root beer. They were all enjoying the fruits of their victory over Clint. The coach made a short speech thanking the team for their effort. The school principal and other dignitaries made longer speeches and talked about the beginning of another winning tradition and other things that Josh paid no attention to. He had lost interest and was tired of people staring at his swollen face. It seemed that everybody who congratulated him had to follow up with a firm pat on the back that only aggravated the pain in his head. Cindy came up to the bandstand. She was still wearing her cheerleader outfit. She put her arm around Josh and whispered in his ear and with a mischievous grin rejoined the other cheerleaders. His teammates watched Cindy walk away with envy and unabashed lust.

"Be glad to handle that for you if you're not feeling up to it." Bryan grinned and punched Josh's arm.

Josh's nose throbbed.

"Go right on 'head, Bryan." Josh thought about punching him back but it wouldn't be worth the pain.

After the speeches the Pep squad cleared the chairs from the main floor and set up the hi-fi. The crowd began filling the dance floor as the records were played non-stop. Josh watched the dancers with little interest and began thinking about going home.

"Hey Josh." Lorenzo, who sat next to him pointed to the dance floor. "Roble keeps sneaking looks at you and you're not even paying attention."

"Row-blay." Lorenzo pronounced the name as it was meant to be pronounced with a slight trill on the "R" and a soft touch on the "b" so that her name floated elegantly in the warm, stuffy air of the community center.

He spotted Roble in the crowd and watched as she danced. A different boy was waiting for the next dance at the end of each song. Roble never rested between songs and never refused anyone a dance.

Josh was surprised by a little stab of jealousy as he watched her. She had the energy of a spirited filly just let out of a corral and she danced and danced like she might not ever be let out again.

Josh was thinking about Missy and how she had promised that she would be at homecoming. He missed her and wished she were here but he couldn't keep his eyes off Roble. She wore Wranglers and boots and a western cut white shirt that made her skin glow. Her black hair swung in soft, shining waves as she danced.

Josh put down his soda, got down off the bandstand and moved over toward Roble. He reached her just as the dance ended. She left her dance partner, ignoring the others, and came over to Josh and took his hand. The next song was a slow one and Josh felt he could manage it without too much pain. Roble hugged him tight, her head against his chest, her eyes closed. Josh shuffled his feet in time to the music. He was not a good dancer and he moved awkwardly to the music. He closed his eyes but had to keep his mouth open so he could breathe. He concentrated on pursing his lips, opening his mouth just a little so he didn't look like a fool. The song ended too quickly and before he could say anything Roble pulled him toward the door.

"C'mon, Josh. Let's get some fresh air."

Josh noticed Cindy's frown as they walked past her and the other cheerleaders.

Roble kept tight hold on his hand and as they went outside the cool air felt good on his face. People were sitting on their cars and trucks in the parking lot drinking and talking. He saw Sue Ann across the lot. She had turned her pickup around and was sitting in the back, legs dangling off the tailgate. She waved them over, a pint bottle in one hand and a cigarette in the other. They went over to her pickup. Sue Ann kidded Josh about his dancing as she sipped regularly from the bottle. They talked about the game and about the rumors of Coach being fired but Josh did not want to relive the game and he figured that the rumors about Coach probably were not true. His face felt puffy and it began to hurt but it was good being there with Roble and he did not want to leave. They sat on Sue Ann's pickup making small talk and watching the crowd come and go. After a while Roble became concerned that her aunt would wonder where she was.

"I'll go check in with my Tia and be right back." She squeezed Josh's hand and walked back to the building.

"Now, there's a pair to draw to!" Sue Ann nodded in the direction of two tall, solidly built young men near the door. The two were watching Roble intently as she approached the building. The larger of the two said something and they both laughed as they kept their eyes on Roble. Roble was either unaware of them or ignored them as she went back inside. The two young men continued to stare at her until she was lost in the crowd.

"Who the hell are they?" Josh asked.

"Real trouble. That's who they are. They're kin to old man Hazen. I heard they're his brother's boys. Anyway they were in jail for beating a woman near to death in east Texas but now they're out and staying at the Hazen place."

"They've been in the café and it gives me the creeps the way they look at me. I talked to the Deputy about them and he's the one told me about their trouble with the law. He's keeping an eye on them but I tell you, Josh, he's gonna have to watch them real close!"

Josh watched as the two drifted off into the shadows behind the Community Center. He was suddenly worried about Roble.

"Relax Josh, I can see her inside talking with her aunt." Sue Ann was reading his mind.

"That little Mexican gal thinks you are *quite* the boy doesn't she?"

"Her name is Roble and she's as American as you and me!" Josh was irritated with Sue Ann.

"Easy, Josh! You know I don't have anything against Mexicans. Besides I've seen that little gal horseback and she can ride damn near as good as me."

Sue Ann was beginning to slur her words. She put her arm around Josh's shoulders.

They watched as Bryan came out of the building with Cindy holding onto his arm. Bryan waved to Josh and Sue Ann, a big smile on his face. Cindy ignored them. Josh sighed.

"Listen to me, Josh. It's none of my business but I'm making it my business." Sue Ann giggled.

"Take hold of that little Mex - - Roble - - and forget about Missy. Missy is gonna do nothing but cause you trouble and heartache." She removed her arm from his shoulder and lit a cigarette.

"I know how women think and I sure as hell know about trouble and heartache. Missy is using you. She likes you cause you're reliable. You're also cute as hell." Sue Ann giggled. "But that ain't never enough for gals like Missy. She'll keep the reliable and steady part but she'll always be looking for excitement. And mostly, in this life, the reliable and steady types don't provide a hell of a lot of excitement. I mean, it ain't that you all are completely dull but…" Sue Ann stopped and looked up to the stars. Josh followed her gaze upwards. The stars were silver in the clear sky. She was quiet for a while, lost in some old memory, and when she looked back at Josh her eyes were brighter, glistening with just a touch of hurt.

"She'll find some sweet talking son of a bitch the exact opposite of you and she'll have her excitement and after that she'll see that Mr. Sweet Talker is just as selfish as she is and there's never enough room in their lives for two selfish people and then she'll come back for some more steady and dependable. And she'll stay until her need for excitement comes 'round then she'll be off again. Your life with someone like Missy will be a real Rolly Coaster ride. But this little Mexican gal - - she's steady and dependable just like you." Sue Ann was beginning to sway a little.

She patted Josh on the back and he ignored the pain it caused in his head. He was thinking about what Sue Ann had said. It was very confusing.

"It's confusing. Ain't it, Josh?" She was reading his mind again.

"Besides, Josh. There's Missy's family. Well, let's look at that shall we?" Sue Ann was shaking her head. "You don't have money and you don't have family. You think they'll ever let Missy have anything even semi-serious to do with you?"

They saw Roble come out of the building and make her way over to them.

"My Tia says we have to go now so I guess I'll have to say goodnight." She held Josh's hand in both of hers and kissed him on the cheek.

"'Bye, Sue Ann." She kissed Sue Ann on both cheeks.

"'Night, Roble." Sue Ann patted her cheek.

Josh walked Roble to the building talking quietly with her and when she went inside he walked back over to Sue Ann. "I gotta go, Sue Ann." His face showed the pain.

"Nose hurtin'?"

"Yeah."

"Here." She grabbed her purse and felt around inside. She pulled out a small glass vial and removed two pills.

"The dentist gave me these last month when he pulled my wisdom teeth. Take one and it'll help you sleep but don't take it 'til you're ready to go to sleep. It's pretty powerful."

"Thanks, Sue Ann."

Sue Ann got down off the bed of her truck and kissed Josh on the cheek.

"Take care, darlin' and stop by the café tomorrow. I'll treat you to breakfast."

"Okay. See you then." Josh walked over to his truck. His head was throbbing and his vision was blurred.

He drove down Main Street, through the center of town and out past the Cotton Gins and turned into the El Paso Red Flame gas station. He parked in back by the storeroom. There was a cot set up in the storeroom and that was where Josh had been sleeping for the past month. He lay down on the cot and he felt like his head would explode. It felt better when he sat up so he remained sitting for a while but he was getting sleepy. He tried lying down again but the pain was too much. He remembered what Sue Ann said about the pill and he washed it down with a cup of water. He grabbed his pillow and all the wool blankets on the cot and walked out to his pickup.

He put the pillow up against the side window of the driver's door and stretched his feet out on the seat. He spread the blankets out over him and leaned back against the pillow. His whole body was starting to relax and go a little numb. He tried to think about what Sue Ann told him about Missy and he also wondered about his feelings for Roble but his thoughts were all tangled up as the pain pill began to take effect. For the first time tonight he was without pain and his mind was not troubled at all. He was a little light-headed but he was at peace and very content and he was smiling as he began dancing a slow dance with Roble.

DRIVING BRACEROS

Carrying their boxes of groceries, the braceros came out of the Emporium and gathered in small groups along the wall of the store to smoke and talk among themselves. The rising moon spilled a long shadow down the side of the building and the tip of their cigarettes glowed in the dark. Several of the men in their stiff, new denim jackets with the collars turned up, leaned against the wall and looked over at the two panel trucks in the dirt lot next to the store. The braceros were waiting for the foreman.

Josh sat in one of the trucks and tried to make the heater work. The truck was only two years old but like everything in the valley it was hard used and looked older. The rubber pads were gone from the pedals, the gearshift knob was broken and one of the heater buttons was missing. Josh twisted the stem of the temperature control with pliers he had dug out from under the seat and immediately felt the heat blast down onto the toes of his boot. He was waiting for the foreman.

The owner of the Emporium also owned the trucks and had learned long ago that left on their own, the braceros would load into trucks with cousins and friends who worked on farms distant from their own and this cost extra fuel and time in their transportation. So the owner hired a foreman, a long-time resident of the valley, who knew every farm in the valley. His job was to group the braceros into the trucks according to the farms they worked. The store owner paid his drivers by the load, not by the hour, so they drove hard trying to get in as many loads as possible each Saturday night during the season.

Josh began driving for the store at the end of last year's harvest. It was only a Saturday job during the harvest but it was easy money and this would be the last trip of the evening and the season.

Guillermo, the Foreman, came out of the store and began directing the groups of braceros to the trucks. He brought eight braceros to Josh's truck and knocked on the window. He was holding a small paper sack. The window glass was stuck in the up position so Josh opened the door.

"Reeves farm and Chavez farm and Señor McCormick wants you to drop this off at the Lazy B. Is for la Señora Smith." Guillermo held the bag looking at Josh as if to make sure he understood before he gave it to him.

"Reeves, Chavez and drop this at the Lazy B," Josh repeated. His heart jumped when he said "Lazy B." He grabbed the bag and put it on the seat next to him and then went around to the back of the truck and opened the double doors.

The men started loading their boxes into the back of the truck. Behind the front seat on each side there were two wooden

94

benches running the length of the truck. The braceros sat on the benches with the boxes between them on the floor and the oldest of the men sat up front with Josh.

When the men and groceries were loaded, Josh closed the doors, got into the driver's seat, pulled the shift lever into low gear and eased out onto Main Street. The old man riding up front put his chin on his chest and would sleep until Josh woke him.

At the crossroads in the middle of town Josh turned west toward Wind Mountain and drove a steady forty-five miles an hour. It was hot in the truck so he cracked the wing window to let in some fresh air. The heater fan only worked on the high setting so he turned it off but could not adjust the temperature without the pliers. The men smoked and talked in the back. They smoked Mexican cigarettes; Faros and Delicados which burned fast and gave off a sweet smell, much different from American cigarettes and the sweet smoke mixed with the smell of dried sweat and garlic. It was a working man's fragrance and Josh liked it, even though he held only part time jobs, it made him feel part of a man's world.

As he reached the end of the blacktop he felt the washboard surface under the wheels and slowed to twenty five miles an hour to prevent the truck from skating across the closely rutted top of the road. Last year while he was going too fast, he had skidded into the bar ditch, spilling groceries and angry Mexicans all over the inside of the truck. The humility of his failure in front of the braceros was still with him and he would not let that happen again. So he kept it at a steady twenty five and followed the power lines and the caliche road, a white path through the creosote out to the western end of the valley.

The moon was well up over Wind Mountain when he dropped off the last bracero at the Chavez farm and headed back to the main road. The Lazy B was five miles further west and he drove fast. Melissa Smith was home from boarding school and he hoped she had not gone to bed. He felt the truck begin to slide on the road but did not slow down. He stayed in the middle of the road and steered lightly. It was hot in the truck but he did not want to stop and try to fix the heater so he turned the wing all the way round and the cold air rushed in over his face and chest.

The caliche road was bright in front of him. The power poles and creosote bushes began to rush by faster and he pushed his foot down harder on the gas pedal. He could not think of anything except getting to the Lazy B before Melissa went to bed. The speed and the wind rushing in through the wing gave him a feeling of freedom and as he neared Yucca hill he increased his speed so that the incline would not slow him down. His heart beat faster. The bright caliche faded into the shadows as the top of the hill hid the moon and the truck's headlights cast strange shadows among the creosote and yuccas.

He felt the rear end of the truck begin to slide to the right. He lightly corrected with the steering wheel and came back up onto the crown of the road. He pushed harder on the gas pedal. As he topped the hill once again it was bright as day and he did not need the truck's lights to see the road. The power poles flew by. The truck slid to the right again and was moving steadily off the crown to the edge of the road. Lightly and slowly he corrected with the steering wheel and the truck straightened and moved back to the center. He pushed the gas pedal to the floor. He was calm and in control now. His heart slowed to normal as the truck picked up speed. The power lines turned sharply south away from the road and now it was just caliche and creosote in the moonlight. The road was a bright ribbon, narrowing as it ran on toward the mountain and then he saw the lights of the Lazy B coming up fast on his right. Very slowly he reduced his speed. He dared not touch the brakes. He took a deep breath and as the truck slowed, he pulled off the main road at the ranch gates and drove slowly up to the house.

The dogs came down off the porch as the truck crossed the cattle guard into the main yard. They barked as he pulled up to the front of the house. He called them by name and they followed him onto the porch sniffing his boots and wagging their tails. He heard piano music then heard it stop when he knocked on the door. Mrs. Smith opened the door, smiled and waved him in. It was warm in the house and the spiced smell of baking reminded him that he had not eaten since breakfast.

"It's Josh," Mrs. Smith announced. The music began again.

"Mr. McCormick asked me to drop this off on my way back to town." He handed her the bag.

She looked into the bag. "Bless his heart he remembered my ginger and Mexican chocolate. Come in and sit down while I fix you a cup of cocoa. "Missy, Josh is here." Her voice was louder this time.

The music stopped and his heart beat faster as Melissa came into the room. "Hi, Josh." She kissed him on the cheek and grabbed both his hands. "Hi, Melissa."

She had cut her hair since he had last seen her on Labor Day and it made her look older. She looked directly into his eyes, smiling at him and not saying a word.

"I heard your music, what is it?" He felt his face burn.

She looked at him, her eyes holding his a moment longer, still quiet. "It's Beethoven," she turned and still holding his hands took him into the living room. "Sit down here by the fire and I'll play for you."

He sat on the hearth feeling the fire on his back and was captive to the sweet, spicy warmth of the baking smells from the kitchen. Melissa sat at the piano and looked at him as she began playing. The melody was beautiful, almost sad, the delicate notes making him wonder at the music. He watched her hands move over the keyboard and felt comfortable by the fire with the music and the baking smells. She continued to look at him like someone she had not seen in a very long time. He felt his stomach growl as the smell of the Mexican cocoa drifted in from the kitchen. He was afraid his stomach could be heard over the music.

"It's the *Moonlight Sonata*." Her eyes were dancing. "I didn't know you liked Beethoven."

He did not know who Beethoven was and he knew she was teasing him but he did not care. He was cozy in the cozy room with the fire and the music and baking and cocoa smells.

He listened as the deep notes played out steady and then the higher notes went running off in a different direction, like they were dancing around the deep notes going away but always coming back and then away again before coming back to be part of the slow, steady march. He was dancing with them. Wandering off.

He was stirred out of his wanderings as the tempo and mood of the music changed to a sharper and more complicated sound. Melissa was concentrating, her eyes on the keyboard. She frowned very slightly and pursed her lips. Her fingers moved quickly over the keyboard as the notes, still delicate but more complex, set a lively cadence and he began moving his fingers against his leg in rhythm.

She finished the last measure and told him the name of the piece but he did not hear it. He just sat hearing the last notes still playing in his head and after a while he realized that he must look foolish sitting there in the silence. Melissa smiled at him and just before he made a complete fool of himself by saying something dumb, Mrs. Smith brought in a tray with cookies and cups of cocoa. She put it on the hearth.

"I have more baking to tend to so you all enjoy the cocoa before Josh has to get back to town," Mrs. Smith looked directly at Josh as she spoke.

They sat on the hearth, the tray between them. He sipped the cocoa and tried not to wolf down the cookies.

"How have you been, Josh?"

"Fine, I mean work and school, you know."

"Mama told me you got hurt in the homecoming game."

"Yeah, but it's okay."

"Broke your nose?"

"Yeah, but Doc Snead set it."

"Joshua! The county Vet! Let me see." She put a hand on each side of his face and turned him to her, examining the slight curve of his nose. Her eyes were dancing again. "A definite improvement I would say," she laughed.

"Blacked both my eyes. It was pretty ugly."

"So I guess you didn't dance with that new girl at the Homecoming Ball. What's her name, the cheerleader?" she teased.

"No I didn't. I thought you were coming back for home-coming."

She looked away, "Had to stay at school, midterms, you know. Did you miss me? Would you have danced with me? I would have danced with you, black eyes, broken nose and all. You would have been my football hero and I would have been your Home-coming Queen and everyone would have looked at us and been green with envy," she was talking fast, not letting him reply. She grabbed his hand. "I promise you I'll make the next home game and then we can go to the dance after the game and we…"

"The season's over, I played my last game and I don't reckon I'll play football again."

"But what about college? Surely you can make the team."

"Yeah, I guess." There was no sense in talking about it.

Mrs. Smith came in from the kitchen holding a small paper sack.

Josh stood up and put his cup on the tray. "I'd better be getting back."

"Oh, Josh! Wait. I'll walk out to the truck with you." Melissa stood up.

"Thanks for the cookies and cocoa, Mrs. Smith."

"You're welcome, Josh, and please take these cookies to Mr. Mc Cormick." She handed him the paper sack.

"Yes, Ma'am, and thanks again."

Mrs. Smith put her hand on his shoulder and held it there, her eyes smiled a bit sadly. "You're welcome here anytime, Josh."

Outside the temperature had dropped. Melissa put on a coat and they stood on the porch. The lawn of dry Bermuda grass was a bright square in the moonlight. He watched an owl fly off

the barn and disappear quickly into the dark of the field across
the yard beyond the irrigation ditch. Melissa grabbed his arm
with both hands and they stepped down off the porch and
walked quickly to the truck.

She got in on the passenger side and lit a cigarette as he
started the truck and waited for the heater to warm up. She
watched him and smoked. They were quiet. She put the cigarette in the ashtray and moved over to him, put her arm around
his neck and kissed him. Her lips were warm and soft and he
could feel her breath and taste the cigarette smoke and smell
the clean scent of soap. He was dizzy and his heart beat faster.
She kept her arms around his neck a while longer and then
moved back to her side of the seat and picked up the cigarette.

"Will you be around next week?"

"Yeah, I'll probably be helping Bobby at the Red Flame."

"I'm going to El Paso tomorrow but will be back on Tuesday.
My roommate and her brother and some of his fraternity brothers
are spending Thanksgiving with us. I'd like you to meet them."

His heart sank. A brother?

"Let's all meet at the Dixie Freeze Wednesday afternoon,
okay?" She put her hand on his knee.

"And Josh, would you--?" She looked away and then quickly
asked, "Are you still sleeping in your truck?" "No, I got a place.
What were you going to ask me?" The porch light flickered on
and off several times.

"I gotta go." She took two quick drags and put the cigarette
in the ashtray. "See you Wednesday." She kissed him quickly,
got out of the truck and ran to the house. She waved and blew
him a kiss as she went into the house.

He felt out of breath, like he had just run a dozen wind sprints. He sat there for a moment, both hands on the wheel and watched as the porch light went out. He reached over and crushed out Melissa's cigarette in the ashtray and then he put the truck in gear, drove over the cattle guard and headed back to town.

He drove slowly on the way back. The scent of soap and cigarette smoke still made him a little dizzy. The town was a sharp outline in the east, the lights dulled by the moon. The red light on the water tower blinked slowly, a beacon guiding him back home. The mountains rose out of the desert beyond the town and the peak of El Capitan stood bright in the moonlight above the lower mountains that grew darker as they dwindled off to the north.

He dropped off the paper sack of cookies and the truck keys at the store, collected his four dollars and began walking home.

He walked down Main Street two blocks and turned right at the Farmall dealership. Behind the equipment shed were several old army surplus shacks. They were one room buildings made of wood framing and tarpaper with good solid roofs and raised wooden floors. He lived in one of them.

He opened the door and was hit with a strong smell of propane gas. He knew immediately that the line to the small floor heater was leaking. He opened the windows, left the door open and went out to the propane tank. He closed the main valve and walked over to his truck. He started the engine and ran the heater while he waited for the gas fumes to blow out of the shack. He would wait until morning to fix the gas line.

He thought about the roommate and her brother and the fraternity brothers. He was not even sure what a fraternity brother was but thought it might have some connection with religion.

After a while he shut off the engine and went back into the shack. The worst of the smell was gone. He closed the door and windows. He kept his coat on and went over to a small wooden table in a corner of the room. There was a metal basin and a bucket half full of water on the table. A thin crust of ice had formed on the water and he broke through this with his bare hand and poured some water into the basin. He had nailed a wooden fruit crate to one of the wall studs above the table and used it to store his shaving things and tooth brush. He brushed his teeth, walked over to the door and spit outside. He decided to not wash his face since he was still shivering from the cold.

He took off his boots but kept on the wool socks and his coat and got into bed. He had four wool army blankets on the bed. Normally he used one to cover the mattress and the other three to cover him during the winter. Tonight, without the heater, he lay on the bare mattress and covered up with all the blankets. A breeze blew out of the north moving the branches of the old Texas Ebony next to the building.

The dry branches scratched against the building in an uneven rhythm. He could see his breath frosting and his nose grew cold. He pulled the blankets up and the felt the rough wool on his face and smelled the old wool smell of the army surplus blankets. He lay there listening to the tree scratching the wall of the building and thought about Melissa and next Wednesday. After a while he pushed the blankets off his face. The table and the wood framing on the walls and ceiling stood out white against the tarpaper in the moonlight. His thoughts faded as sleep came but just before he drifted off he could hear soft, delicate notes being played on a piano.

THE EL PASO
RED FLAME GAS STATION

Sue Ann put the Lone Star Café Sunday Breakfast Special on the counter in front of Josh. His mouth watered as he looked at the full stack of pancakes with two fried eggs on top and sausage on the side.

"You ever work for Jim Arbuckle?" Sue Ann asked.

"No."

"Well, he's looking for some hands to build fence this week. Could be a five or six day job. Interested?"

"Damn straight."

"Thought so. He'll be in here about noon with the rest of the church crowd. I'll tell him about you if you want."

"You bet and I'll be here before noon."

"You doin' okay?" Sue Ann put both hands on the counter and brought her head level with his.

"Yeah, I'm fine."

"You still sleeping in your truck?"

"No. I'm renting a place from old man Franklin."

"Well, all right then." She picked her cigarette up from the corner of the counter and went over to the coffee urn.

Josh ate slowly and watched her. He sipped water as he ate, he always saved the coffee for after, drawing out the meal.

He watched Sue Ann work behind the counter, sweeping platters off the pass-through from the kitchen, checking order slips, talking to the cook and the customers, grabbing her cigarette from the ashtray, taking quick puffs before setting it back and moving on to the next task. She made coffee, filled sugar bowls, carried dirty dishes back to the kitchen and took money at the cash register. Moving all the time, talking, letting some flirtatious remarks slide by, catching others and throwing them right back to the farmers and ranch hands that made them.

She moved with the athletic grace of the All-District basketball star she had been. She still wore her hair in a ponytail and the years did not take away a bit of her competitive spirit. Without seeming to, she was aware of everything in the café and moved in anticipation of a customer's need. Old boyfriends and old farmers watched her with different kinds of regret but were always polite and very protective of her on rare occasions when a rude ranch hand or fresh stranger stepped over the line.

Josh reckoned he had been in love with her since the first time he saw her.

He ate slowly and watched her. He sopped up the last of the syrup and egg yolk with the last of the pancakes and then began sipping his coffee.

The café began to empty and she came back to stand between him and the coffee pots and began filling salt shakers.

She pulled a fresh cigarette out of her apron pocket, pulled a pot off the burner and poured some coffee into his cup. Refills cost five cents but she never charged him. She held the coffee pot looking at him for a few seconds then turned and went back to the kitchen. She came back carrying a small plate with two pieces of buttered toast and put it in front of him and took the empty Sunday Special platter away. She put a small container of jelly next to the toast and poured him some more coffee.

"I don't have enough…" He looked at the toast.

She cut him off with a look and went over to the cash register to ring up a customer.

Sue Ann came back and filled his water glass.

"Missy's home. She was in yesterday evening."

"I know. I saw her last night."

She looked at him, her eyes questioning.

"I mean - - at her place. While I was delivering braceros. I had to drop something off from the Emporium."

"College girl!" She huffed.

He swallowed some water, "Not college. An academy. She goes to a boarding school but they call it an academy."

"Uh huh, that figures." She blew a long stream of smoke at him.

"You goin' to college, too?" She put her cigarette down and before he could answer she said, "No. I reckon you're gonna have a hard enough time gettin' out of high school." she chuckled.

He sat for a while, finishing his coffee and then he got up and walked over to the cash register. He gave Sue Ann two dollars and she gave him back his change.

"Remember Mr. Arbuckle at noon."

"I'll be here."

She was already pouring coffee at a table when he walked out to his truck. He pulled out his billfold and counted the few bills in it. He had four dollars and change left. Enough for some gas and a couple of meals if he was careful, but if he got on with Mr. Arbuckle, he would have enough to get him to Christmas.

Bobby was at the island of the El Paso Red Flame gas station, bent over the front tire of Johnny's bicycle when Josh pulled up next to the gas pumps. He got out of the truck and pulled the cap off the gas tank.

"Hi, Bobby, Hi, Johnny. You get the reading off this pump?"

"Yeah, go 'head." Bobby was attaching a cut piece of oil can to the front fork of Johnny's bike.

Josh turned the crank on the pump until the cash and gallon columns rolled around to zero and then began pumping gas into his truck.

Johnny had two small red wagons tied in tandem behind his bike. There were empty beer and soda bottles in the wagons and Josh noted that many of the bottles were broken.

"Hey, Johnny, when did you start picking up broken bottles?"

Johnny was quiet not taking his eyes off Bobby and Josh noticed a couple of fresh bandages on his face and some gauze wrapped around his left hand.

"Nobody's going to buy broken beer bottles, Johnny," Josh teased.

"One thousand nine hundred and thirty nine," Johnny said

"Johnny took a spill." Bobby said. He stood up and checked the wire clamp that held the stiff piece of oil can firm against the spokes of the bike's front wheel.

"Take her out for a spin and see how that works and then come on around back with those bottles." Bobby told Johnny.

Josh stopped the pump at three gallons and put the nozzle back in its slot. He stepped across the island to look at Bobby's handiwork.

Johnny shuffled over to Josh.

"Bobby fix juck." He smiled. Johnny was most always smiling.

"Yeah, looks like Bobby did a real fine job."

"Go on, Johnny, take her for a spin and don't forget to bring them bottles around the back." Bobby held the bike by the handlebars.

Johnny got on the bike and pedaled off in the direction of the cotton gin, the piece of oil can stuttering against the spokes and the bottles rattling in the wagons.

They turned and walked into the office. Josh handed Bobby a dollar bill and he rang up the sale on the cash register. There was a quart of buttermilk, a pack of cigarettes and an open first-aid kit on the counter next to the register.

Bobby gave Josh his change, picked up the buttermilk and took two big gulps. He sat on the stool next to the register and lit a cigarette. He began putting the iodine and bandages back in the kit.

"Any work come in?" Josh asked.

"Just a couple of flats and a valve job. Even the gas business is slow. I heard that old man Arbuckle is putting a crew together to build some fence on his place."

"Yeah. Sue Ann told me about it this morning. I'm going to see him around noon and try to get on."

"Well, he's a tough old cob but he pays cash."

"That's what I'm countin' on."

Johnny grimaced and drank more buttermilk.

"Ulcer acting up?" Josh asked.

"Not too bad." He took a deep drag on the cigarette. "How you doin'?"

"Okay. If I can get on with Arbuckle, I'm good through Christmas."

"Well, if old man Franklin kicks you out of your place, your cot is still set up in the store room. I slept there last week after too much whiskey. Colder'n a whore's heart but it's yours if you need it. No need to go back to sleepin' in your truck."

"Thanks. Appreciate it."

They heard the rattle of Johnny's wagons and the light drone of the metal on spokes as Johnny rode up out back. Bobby got some change out of the register and Josh followed him out to the back of the building.

Johnny had his bike propped against an old fifty-five gallon oil drum and was polishing the handle bars with a shop rag.

Bobby checked the piece of oil can on the front fork and bent the sides of the thin metal to stiffen it. He then went back to the wagons and knelt down to look at the bottles.

"Okay, Johnny, let's count the bottles."

"One thousand, nine hundred and thirty nine," Johnny said. He put the rag in his back pocket and knelt down next to Bobby.

"No, I count twenty three." Bobby said. "Let's see – at two cents a piece how much does that make?"

"One thousand, nine hundred and thirty nine." Johnny started scooping the bottles into a cardboard box next to the oil drum.

"No. That's forty six cents and don't be touchin' them broken ones."

"Okay, Bobby."

Josh came over and helped Bobby empty the broken glass from the wagons.

Bobby gave Johnny five nickels and twenty-five pennies.

Johnny held the change in his bandaged hand and with his right hand began putting the coins, one at a time, into the right front pocket of his pants. He squinted his eyes and stuck his tongue between his teeth concentrating as he counted out each coin.

Bobby scooped the last of the broken glass out of the bottom of the wagons with a piece of cardboard and watched Johnny finish counting the last of the change. When Johnny finished he clapped his hands together as if brushing off dust. One thousand, nine hundred and thirty nine," He said.

"Okay now, Johnny, I ain't buyin' no broken bottles no more. Understand?"

"Okay, Bobby."

"Now get your juck on down the road. Back to work."

"Okay, Bobby."

Josh watched Johnny as he rode his bike out past the cotton gins, toward town. "I always wondered if that was the only number he knows."

Bobby shook his head. "Nineteen thirty nine, the year he was born. It *is* the only damn number he knows."

He looked at Josh. "The Hazen boys ran him into a bar ditch this mornin'. That's how come them broken bottles. Susie Holguin saw the whole thing. Said the Hazen boys were laughin' like hell. I talked to Susie and asked her not to tell Johnny's folks 'bout what happened. I'm afraid Johnny's old man would go after those two boys and then we'd have a killin'. Appreciate if you don't say anything. I'll just tell him that Johnny took a spill." Bobby stepped on his cigarette and twisted it to shreds with his boot. "That's just puredee meanness, 'specially of a Sunday." They watched Johnny cross over main street and pedal out of sight behind the Electric Coop building, and then they walked back to the office, carrying the unbroken bottles and Bobby began putting them into a wooden case next to the soda machine. Josh grabbed a push broom and went out to the shop. He spent an hour sweeping the floor and cleaning the shop while Bobby worked on the books in the office.

He had finished servicing the hydraulic lift and was cleaning his hands when he heard the rumbling exhaust of a new Chevrolet V-8 pull up to the island.

A horn honked twice. "Hey, Bobby get your skinny ass out here." The Hazen boys didn't have respect for anyone.

Josh walked up to the front of the shop and saw Bobby cross over in front of the Chevy and stand at the end of the island between the pumps and the air hose.

"What do you boys want?" Bobby asked.

"What the hell you think? Fill it with Ethyl and check the oil." The older boy said.

"No." Bobby stood with his arms crossed, his hands holding his sharp elbows. "You're not getting' anything here." He spoke slowly, watching the older brother.

The younger brother opened the passenger door. "What the hell you talkin' about?"

"Billy, don't get out of the car!" Bobby said, his voice louder now.

The older brother was smarter and more cunning. "What's goin' on Bobby?"

"Ya'll ran Johnny into a bar ditch this mornin' and you won't do business here until you apologize to him and pay him for the bottles you broke."

Josh stepped back into the shop and grabbed a twelveinch crescent wrench from the work bench, slipped it into his back pocket and walked to the front of the shop.

"And when I tell the boys down at the Humble station about Johnny, you won't get no gas there neither," Bobby said.

The younger brother stepped out of the car and started in Bobby's direction but stopped when he saw Josh come out of the shop and stand in front of the office.

Billy screamed across the car at Bobby. "I'll kick your skinny ass!"

Josh pulled the crescent out of his back pocket and held it tightly against the side of his right leg and stepped off the walk onto the driveway. His mouth was dry and his heart was pounding. Billy saw him move and hesitated. All his attention was now on Josh.

Bobby spoke calmly, his arms still crossed. "There won't be no ass kickin' today. Eddy, tell your little brother to get back in the car.

Eddy spoke in a flat tone to his brother. "Get back in the car."

Billy hesitated.

"Get back in the goddam car!" Eddy yelled.

Eddy had a thin smile on his face, looking at Bobby the whole time.

Billy got back in the car, his eyes on Josh. It had been a long time since Josh had seen eyes so full of hate. Billy was an explosion waiting to happen but until that time he would dole out misery in small measures.

Eddy gunned the Chevy and left a streak of rubber as he squealed out of the driveway, fishtailing on the dirt between the station and the road, squealing the tires again as he slid onto the blacktop and sped south out of town.

Bobby walked back to the office, his arms still folded across his chest. His face was pale and there was sweat on his face. He picked up the buttermilk and began to drink but stopped and sat down on the stool. "You Okay, Bobby?"

"Yeah, watch the front for a minute." Bobby went around the side to the restroom. Josh heard him coughing and retching and then he heard the water run in the sink.

Bobby wasn't as pale when he came back into the office. He picked up the quart bottle and drank off most of the buttermilk.

"You better get down to the café and catch Arbuckle before he takes on another hand." Bobby was looking up at the office clock. It was quarter of twelve.

"All right. I'll be back after I talk to him."

He walked around to the restroom to comb his hair and clean up. He noticed the blood in the sink and on the wall over the sink. He wet some paper towels and cleaned it up. He would not mention it to Bobby and he didn't want anyone else to see it. He was worried about Bobby but knew better than to push him about the ulcer.

He washed up and combed his hair and thought about the Hazen boys and the trouble they would cause him.

The parking lot of the Lone Star was filled with the vehicles of the church crowd so Josh parked down the street in front of the Boll Weevil bar and walked back to the café. He saw Arbuckle's pickup in the lot and went over to stand under a big cottonwood and wait.

Jim Arbuckle was a big man with a slow deliberate walk, picking each spot carefully before he put his foot down. He held the door open for his wife and held her elbow as she came down the steps.

"Mr. Arbuckle?" Josh stepped from under the tree.

"Hello, Josh. Sue Ann said you'd be here."

"Yessir."

"You still work for Bobby down at the Red Flame?"

"I'll wait for you in the truck, darlin'" Mrs. Arbuckle smiled at Josh and walked towards the truck.

"No, sir. Only in the busy season. It's kinda slow now."

"You ever build fence?"

"Yessir."

"Who for?"

"Ed Mather."

"When?"

"Last summer."

Mr. Arbuckle looked into Josh's eyes his clear blue eyes penetrating, commanding. "What do you do when you come to a ninety in the fence line?"

Arbuckle's jaw was set, his mouth a thin line. Josh felt like Arbuckle was trying to bore through his head with his eyes.

"You plant a brace post and a dead man after the last post, pull the wire taut with the block and tackle before you make your turn." Josh looked back into Arbuckle's eyes.

Mr. Arbuckle continued to stare at Josh for a moment longer, then his face relaxed and he turned, looking across the street. "Well, you'll probably only be working the crow bar and setting posts. That suit you?"

"Yessir."

"We start tomorrow morning and plan to finish next Saturday." He pulled a pocket watch out of his shirt pocket. "I pay ten dollars a day, give you room and board Monday through Friday. Come up tonight if you want, but no supper. If you all finish by Friday evening I pay half-day's bonus."

He closed the watch and put it back in his pocket. "My fence will be straight or nobody gets paid. Any time spent fixing mistakes is on you. I don't pay for others' mistakes."

"Yessir."

"Okay. If you come up tonight, see Enrique in the little house just inside the last cattle guard. He'll show you where to bunk.

"Yessir. Thanks, Mr. Arbuckle."

Arbuckle started toward his truck but stopped and turned. "Oh, Josh!" He walked back in Josh's direction.

"Yessir?"

"That was a hell of a catch you made in the Clint game."

"Thanks, but if you remember the linebacker slipped. That made it easy."

"It was a pleasure to watch, we hadn't beat Clint in four years.

He watched Josh closely. "Your folks must have been proud."

Josh felt his face burning. His jaws tightened. He searched Arbuckle's face looking for the mockery, the teasing. "I don't believe I know your folks."

Josh studied Arbuckle. Listening for the tone in his voice. He could always pick out the tone. People had a hard time hiding it. He found none. Arbuckle's eyes were clear and honest.

"No, sir. They're not from around here."

"Oh." Arbuckle turned back to his truck. "Breakfast tomorrow morning at six."

Josh waited until the Arbuckles pulled out of the lot and turned north on Main before he went over to the café and waved at Sue Ann through the plate glass window.

She winked and smiled back at him from behind the cash register.

He took his toothbrush and shaving gear from the shelf above the wash basin and put it into his dopp kit. He went over to the bed and pulled his work boots and gloves from under it and took down an old pair of Wranglers and work shirt from the shelf. He put it all in a canvas grip and started out the door to his truck but stopped and came back to the closet. All that remained in the closet was a new pair of Wranglers and one good shirt. He took them out, deciding he would leave them at the station with Bobby for safekeeping. He rolled the wool blankets on the bed into a bedroll and tied it with an old belt. He took all of it out to the truck and went back and closed the door to the shack.

When Josh pulled up to the pumps, Bobby was in the shop working on a flat truck tire that was face down under the hydraulic lift.

"I got on!" Josh said.

"Glad to hear it!" Bobby was carefully holding the air nozzle clear of the safety rim in case it blew off as he filled the tire.

"I need to fill up and pay you when I get back."

"Go 'head." Bobby was squatting over the lift, his bony knees around his ears, listening closely to the air hiss into the tire, hoping the tire bead would close evenly on the split rim. "And take a couple of cans of thirty weight too."

Josh filled the truck with gas and took his good clothes around back to the storeroom. He hung them on a hook and locked up and went back out front to the office.

Bobby had taken two quarts of oil from the shelf and put them on the counter. He looked tired. He sat on the stool and lit a cigarette. Josh wrote out a ticket and put it in the cash register.

"Bobby, I, uh, well, I was supposed to see Missy at the Dixie Freeze on Wednesday and now, well, if she comes in would you tell her 'bout the job?"

"Yeah, okay." Bobby held the cigarette in the corner of his mouth while he opened a bottle of buttermilk.

"I was gonna ask Sue Ann but…"

Bobby just looked at him and gulped the buttermilk. "You want me to tell her anything special or give her a love letter or maybe sing her a love song?" He grinned.

Josh grinned back. "No thanks." He picked up the oil.

"Gotta go. See you Saturday or maybe Friday evening."

"I'll be right here. I ain't goin' nowhere."

It started to snow early Saturday morning as Josh drove down the mountain from Arbuckle's place and by the time he made the flats the snow thinned to flurries. It thickened again as he drove up Greasewood Pass.

It had been a good crew and they finished the fence to Mr. Arbuckle's satisfaction late Friday evening and Mrs. Arbuckle had even brought them some Turkey and trimmings to the bunk house Thanksgiving evening. Josh held the steering wheel tenderly, his hands were blistered from working the crow bar. He always felt a little sad at the end of a job. He felt the same way at the end of football season, like it was the end of a good thing that might not be as good the next time.

He drove on and watched the snow blow across the road and drift in piles against the rocks in the pass. It was a dry snow and was not sticking to the road but it was thick and he could not see more than a hundred feet ahead. It thinned again as he made his way down the pass and came nearer to Dog Canyon.

He thought of the fifty-five dollars in his billfold and was happy. He thought about Missy and was anxious to see her before she went back to school. He would clean up and change at the station, get a bite to eat and then drive out to her place. He remembered Missy's roommate and her brother and hoped they had left right after Thanksgiving.

He would ask her out for a hamburger and the picture show. He knew he should have asked her last Saturday but this thing with her roommate and the brother flustered him.

It stopped snowing before he reached the State line but the wind was cold and he kept the heater on full blast until he reached his house.

Josh grabbed his bedroll and grip and went into the house. He stopped just inside the door and looked at the bed. The mattress was gone! He looked around the room. It was gone! The small, round springs of the cot were hooked into the holes at the foot and head and down each side of the metal frame and he could see the baling wire in the middle where he had replaced some missing springs. He stood there for a moment, confused, and then he put the bedroll and grip on the bed and sat on the edge. He sat for a while, looking out the door and running his fingers slowly over the tightly stretched springs. He took a long, deep breath and wondered about the mattress. Why would someone take it? Who? It was army surplus, old and lumpy. It came with the bed and couldn't be much use to anyone. He sat for a while longer suddenly feeling very tired. Then he took his bedroll and clothes back out to the pickup and drove over to the Red Flame.

Bobby was in the back of the shop working on the valve grinder. He turned, saw Josh and switched off the machine. He grabbed a shop rag and they both went into the office. Josh handed Bobby a ten dollar bill and Bobby opened the cash register and handed Josh back his ticket and his change. Bobby looked pale, almost gray. He sat on the stool and lit a cigarette.

"Welcome back," He said.

"Thanks. Is the offer still good on the cot out back?"

"Sure. Old man Franklin run you off?"

"No. Someone took my mattress."

"What?"

"Someone took my mattress."

Bobby looked at him. "They take anything else?"

"No. There was nothing else there. Just the mattress."

Bobby puffed on his cigarette and didn't say anything. He got up and walked over to the front window. He looked out at the driveway and pump island.

"I just need to stay here until I can find another mattress."

Bobby stared out the front window of the station. His arms were crossed and his hands were cupped around his elbows.

"Puredee meanness!" he almost whispered. "You know who done it." It was a statement not a question.

"Yeah. I got a pretty good idea," Josh said.

"Just - by - God meanness!" Bobby put the cigarette down in the ashtray.

"Well. Not much I can do. Can't prove it and damn sure can't sleep on the frame."

"Yeah. You're right. I gotta go into El Paso on Monday. Want me to stop by the surplus store and pick up a mattress? Or do you know where you can find another one?"

"No I don't, so if you can do that I'd appreciate it." He was feeling better about the mattress now but he had other troubled thoughts that he could not quite pin down. The thought about driving out to the Lazy B pushed these thoughts out of his mind and brightened his mood.

" I gotta get cleaned up and change. It's Saturday and I just got paid." He laughed. "Come on, Bobby. Close this place down and let's go get a hamburger!"

"Naw, I ain't hungry. 'Sides, I gotta finish that valve job."

Josh went out to his truck and got his shaving kit and a towel and then went around the side to the men's room. He shaved and cleaned up, went around back to the storeroom and put on his good clothes and boots.

Bobby was back at the valve grinder.

"Did Missy come in while I was gone?" Josh was running a comb through his hair.

"Yeah." Bobby spoke loudly over the low groan of the machine. "They came in yesterday in two cars. Some other girl and a couple of guys. Looked like college kids. She asked about you so I told her where you were and when you was coming back."

"I'm headin' out to her place after I grab a burger at the Lone Star."

Bobby switched off the valve grinder and turned around.

"Josh. When they came in here they filled up. They was headin' back to El Paso."

Bobby saw the look on Josh's face and he turned back to the machine. He would not tell Josh that the college boy was laughing with Missy in his sporty little car and that there was no doubt in Bobby's mind that he was more than just a friend. Not the way they were looking at each other.

"Said to tell you she had to go back early. Said she would see you Christmas."

Josh stood there looking at Bobby's back. His mind was running full speed but his thoughts made no sense and it was like he was trying to catch his balance. He stood there for a while and then realized he probably looked like a fool standing there with his comb in his hand. The valve grinding machine growled and Bobby adjusted some knobs changing the pitch of the sound as more metal was removed from the valve. Josh put the comb in his pocket and turned and walked out of the shop toward his pickup. Then he stopped and looked at the truck for a moment and came back into the shop. He went over and grabbed the push broom and beginning at the back of the shop he swept slowly and deliberately to the front. He pushed the broom in straight rows, his hands still tender from the crow bar.

Bobby switched off the machine. "Hey! I thought you was gonna go to chow!"

Josh kept sweeping, looking at the floor. "Nah! I ain't hungry."

He swept from back to front, making small piles of dirt at the front of the shop and when he had swept up all the dirt, he walked slowly to the back and pushed the broom to the front again in slow strokes, the rhythm becoming steady. He concentrated, not thinking beyond each deliberate stroke. The stiff bristles of the broom made crisp hissing sounds as they moved over the uneven concrete. He gripped the broom tighter and the blisters split open and his hands burned and he felt the blister fluid run down his hand over his fingers. He gripped harder. The burning and the steady, measured hisses of the broom filled his mind.

Bobby switched the valve grinder on again and the growl of the machine covered the sound of the broom.

Josh didn't notice. He kept on sweeping.

AN UNDERSTANDING

Josh was silent simply because he did not know what to say. If asked he would not have been able to describe his feelings. A bit lost or like losing something would be close to it.

Finally he said:

"I don't understand why you want to leave."

"Oh, Josh. Of all people I thought you would understand." She looked at him; she seemed tiny and a bit fragile. "I am the first in my family who has ever been offered a scholarship. Can't you see what this means to me? I have worked hard for this and I cannot, will not, let this chance pass me by."

Josh walked away from her, across the flat to the creek. Everyone called this place Green Meadow even though it wasn't green and not a real meadow but just a piece of flat ground between the stand of cedar on one side and the cliffs on the other side of the creek. No grass grew there nor any plants for that matter. It was just packed dirt and rocks. A spot where the creek descended through the high boulders and ran straight before falling off in a gentle slope to the flats below. The water ran over smooth rocks and on the cliff side backed into some shallow pools in the shade of the towering rock. The sky had gone from a clear light blue to a dull gray with clouds building over the flats. It was early spring but the winds gusting from the north still had a cold winter's bite. Josh knew that in a while the gusts would become a steady blow and bring rain. It was too late in the season for snow but the rain would be cold and he knew they should be getting back to his pickup truck.

She walked slowly over to the creek, about twenty yards downstream. She wore his football letter jacket. He had given it to her shortly after it was awarded to him by the Athletic Association which was a group of merchants and farmers who chipped in and bought the jackets for the high school athletes who had earned their letters. Giving your girl your senior ring or a letter jacket was the accepted fad that acknowledged a steady relationship. Josh did not have the money to buy his senior ring so he had given Roble his letter jacket. The thought of her going away to college in Austin upset and confused him. Bobby had promised him a full-time job at the Red Flame gas station when he graduated in a couple of months. He had plans to supplement his salary at the Red Flame by hauling alfalfa for one of the Valley farmers which would provide enough income to rent a decent place.

He walked over to where she stood and together they watched the water flow down the slope. The clouds had cut the sun light and the water did not sparkle but rippled downstream without color.

"I already told you about my plans," He said

She turned and looked at him with her eyes clear and honest as always. "Yes, Josh. Those plans are fine for you but I have always wanted to make my own plans. I have not kept that from you. I want to get out of the valley and do something else with my life."

"Do those plans include me?" He immediately regretted his words. They made him sound weak, as if he were pleading. He clamped his jaw together.

"Of course they include you. I have never thought of anyone else. But Josh it cannot be here. There is nothing here for me except working for my father at the ranch." She turned to him and took his hand. "Josh. My family has owned land in Texas since it was a Republic. They have bought land and sold it and then bought more and the family has been tied to that land ever since. Cattle, horses and good land is in our blood and has always been our way of life. But I want something different. I will always come back to help out gathering cattle and with other work but I have dreamed of being a doctor since I was little and now have that chance."

Josh looked up at the sky. "We'd best be getting back to the truck."

She held onto his hand all the way back to the truck. After they got in and Josh started it up he let the engine run for a while. He pulled the heater lever to start the water flowing from the engine to the heater core. They sat in silence and felt the wind pick up and begin to batter the truck.

"My father was very upset and was against me going off to college. He did not think his daughter should go out into the world without a man. But my mother and my tia had a long talk with him and he eventually changed his mind although he tried to talk me into going to veterinary school." She grinned.

Josh grunted and busied himself with the heater, not looking at her, then began the drive down to the flats. The heater began throwing out hot air and as the inside of the cab began to fill with heat Roble took off Josh's letter jacket, folded it neatly and placed it on the seat between them.

The first drops of rain fell just as they turned off the dirt road onto the black top that led back to the valley.

CON BENDIGAS DE DIOS

T he Greyhound bus out of El Paso slowed at the junction and then pulled off the Carlsbad highway onto the driveway of the boarded up Fina gas station. A battered, older model pick-up truck sat idling in the cold dawn under the faded blue of the big Fina sign. The driver's window was partially open and cigarette smoke drifted out and up to the sign. The bus driver pulled the emergency brake on and leaned over to the sleeping passenger on the front seat nearest the door. He gently touched the passenger's shoulder. "Wake up, buddy. This is your stop."

Josh came awake, looked at the driver and then stood and reached to the overhead to retrieve his sea-bag. The driver picked up two large, six sided, metal cans from behind his seat, each containing the reels of film for the picture show in town. He set them down outside the bus. Josh swung down from his seat onto the bus steps and grabbed the third can on his way out. He put it down next to the other two. The driver went back into the bus and picked up a bundle of newspapers held together with wire and set it down next to the cans of film. He came over and shook Josh's hand.

"Good Luck," he said and then turned, got into the driver's seat, released the brake and drove back onto the highway. Josh watched as the bus picked up speed, going downhill, heading east to the mountains. The sun had not yet made it over El Capitan but the eastern sky was bright blue with a dinge of orange bouncing off the low clouds hanging around the peak.

"Goddam, it is Josh! Thought that was you got off the bus with the driver. Damn, when did you get back?" The driver of the pickup, cigarette hanging from the corner of his mouth, walked over toward Josh.

"Howdy, Luke. Gimme a ride to town?"

"Damn straight! Good to see you, Josh." They shook hands.

Josh slung his sea-bag over his shoulder and picked up two of the film cans, walked over and put them into the bed of the truck. He looked over at the boarded up gas station.

"When did they close this down?"

"Last year." Luke put the third can into the bed, opened the door and threw the newspapers onto the front seat. "Get in. I got the heater runnin'."

Josh put his sea-bag in the back and got into the cab. Luke pulled out of the driveway, crossed the highway and began the drive into town. Josh settled in, knowing that the trip would take twice as long because Luke never drove over thirty miles per hour.

"Mind helping me roll newspaper?" Luke asked.

"Tell you what, I'll roll them and you drive, okay?" Josh knew that Luke had a tendency to drift off into the bar ditch on a regular basis and he wanted him to concentrate on driving him safely into town.

"Okay, here's a box of rubber bands. And be sure to leave ten unrolled. Five for the Emporium and five for the drug store."

Neither of them spoke as Luke drove along at a steady thirty miles per hour, puffing away at one smoke after another. Josh worked on the newspapers, putting each tightly wrapped paper on the floor of the truck. The sun was higher over the mountains, lighting up the mesa and bringing the creosote and mesquite out of the shadow light turning them into clearly defined forms as the truck rolled steadily north to the valley and town.

Josh caught Luke looking at his uniform and the ribbons on the left side of his blouse. Josh had worn his Class As all the way from San Diego because there was always a chance of running into a bus driver who respected the uniform and who would let him ride free. It finally worked on the last leg from El Paso to the junction which saved him only a few bucks. "You fixin' to come back to stay?" Luke asked.

"Don't know yet."

"Lots of things changed in the valley. A bunch of farmers have done moved off. Blamed the low price of cotton. Say it's not worth growing it no more. Two of the gins shut down."

"How 'bout Bobby?" Josh asked.

"He had to go to Houston 'cause of his sickness and he's still there. I guess nobody knew how sick Bobby was. Hell, even Bobby didn't know. I guess he's doin' okay, though. And that Smith gal that you was sweet on has went back east to school.

Damn she's pretty! And Etienne, the deputy, well, he's over in New Mexico now. Him and his brother, you remember old Jean Pierre? Well they took over their old man's sheep outfit. Oh, yeah, The El Paso Red Flame is closed down."

Josh took this all in as they poked along the road and he finished up folding the newspapers. He looked out over the mesa to the mountains. The sun was clear of the mountain range, streaming in through the passenger side window. He felt its warmth but he did not feel as good as he thought he would as he returned to the only real home he ever had. It sure sounded like the valley had changed since he left for the war but he was truly beginning to understand that he had changed too. Probably even more than the valley. "I heard you was shot twice over there." "What?" Josh was lost in his thoughts.

"I said I heard they shot you twice in Viet Nam."

"I was shot once and then got wounded by a grenade."

"At the same time?"

"No, not at the same time." Josh did not want to talk about it. Not that it caused him any concern; he had gotten over that shortly after he had healed. It was just that he didn't like talking about it to anyone except the Marines who had been there with him. And now that he had told Luke, everyone in the Valley would hear about it, most likely with a lot of exaggeration.

He had been shot while on a patrol. It was a clear hot Wednesday, six months into his tour and a little after lunch. Nothing heroic or remarkable. He made the mistake of standing up and out from cover and the enemy put a bullet into him. The bullet hit his magazine pouch and probably saved his life. But the bullet and several pieces of metal from the magazine tore into his left leg. He spent a month in a hospital in Japan and then they promoted him to Corporal and he returned to his old squad.

Two months later during a firefight near a small village he was wounded by shrapnel from a grenade. They sent him back to the hospital because two of the fragments of metal cut through some nerves in his right leg. When he returned to his squad the second time, his Captain assigned him to staff duty and kept him out of the field.

A small herd of cows was moving off a low hill to his right and he watched their ambling gait as they came down to a bare flat piece of ground that sloped into a large draw. Two mounted men appeared from behind the hill and rode steady on each side of the herd. He could tell from the way they were all moving that they were headed for an old cattle tank which was out of sight from the road but he remembered it from a summer he had spent working this ranch. He watched the cowboys and their slow, easy pace as they kept the herd from spreading out. He probably knew these old boys but was too far away to recognize them. He missed ranch work and had thought of it often while overseas, but it became more real now that he was back. He could feel the horse beneath him and could smell the dust, the cows and the horse sweat. It brought something to life inside him.

"I forgot to tell ya that ol' Rip got to drinking too much and it got the best of him and they had to send him to some Army hospital in San Antonio to dry out."

"How long's he been there?"

"'Bout a couple a months, I guess."

They were quiet for a while and Josh watched the herd and the two riders go out of sight as they moved down the draw toward the cattle tank.

"How 'bout Roble? She still around?"

"No, she left a couple a months after you did. Went to Austin to some school. Goin' to be a nurse is what I hear." He looked over at Josh. "I forgot you was kinda sweet on her." He grinned. "I always kinda liked her 'cause she could hold her own with any rowdy cowboy when we was gatherin' cows at her daddy's place. As good as she was horseback, I always reckoned she would take up barrel racin' but she never did. Tough ol' gal and real pretty too." He watched Josh for his reaction.

Josh stared at the road as it slowly came at them. Luke thought that Josh was moodier than he had ever seen him. Maybe it was just coming home and all.

They came to the end of the high mesa and began the descent into the valley. The trees that were planted years ago as wind breaks throughout the valley were bright green in their new foliage and the spring planting of alfalfa was taking hold, making green squares on the valley floor.

The cotton, what was left of it, would not come up for a month or so but then it would add another shade of green and the valley, in summer, would appear as a lush green oasis to anyone coming in off the creosote and mesquite of the south mesa cow country. Josh's spirits rose. He felt better than he had in a long while and was thankful for Luke's slow driving habits as he watched the valley spread out before him. He was home.

Luke stopped the truck at the pump island of the Texaco station.

"Thanks for the ride, Luke."

"Good to see you again, Josh." They shook hands and Josh carried his sea-bag into the station.

"Howdy, Josh." Mr. Pierce came from behind the counter and shook Josh's hand, "glad you're back safe and sound."

"Howdy, Mr. Pierce."

Josh put his sea-bag on the floor against the counter.

"I was wondering if I could change my clothes here before I headed over to the Lone Star."

Mr. Pierce held his hand up. "Just a sec, Josh." He turned and went behind the parts bins and returned holding two clothes hangers with a shirt, a pair of jeans and he carried a pair of battered Tony Lama boots. "When they closed down the Red Flame and laid Bobby off, he brung these down here. He asked me if I'd keep 'em for you. He brought your pick-up too. Told me he knew you was comin' back. I been usin' it to chase parts in El Paso and Carlsbad. Had Arthur put new rings and bearings in it and rebuild the starter and generator. Bobby had done put new tires on it at the Red Flame. Appears that they didn't care 'bout the inventory when they closed down so he took five new tires and put 'em on your truck. I got it over in the third bay. Hope you don't mind me usin' it but I hated to see it just set there."

"No sir, Mr. Pierce. I appreciate you taking care of it.

Can I change in the backroom?"

"Go right on ahead, Josh."

Josh came back into the office in his old civilian clothes, carrying his class As on a hanger. He picked up his sea-bag and went through the interior door out into the garage bays.

"Howdy, Arthur." Arthur had his head under the hood of a pickup truck.

"Howdy, Josh, welcome home." He wiped his hands on a rag and shook hands with Josh. "Your pickup's over there.

She's runnin' real fine."

"Thanks, Arthur."

Old man Pierce came through the door. "Josh, don't know what your plans are but Arthur and me could sure use another hand and would be proud if you'd consider working for me."

"Thanks, Mr. Pierce, but I was hopin' to get on at a ranch." He saw the disappointment in the old man's eyes. "But yours is the first and only offer I got so let me think on it. I'll let you know today."

"Okay, Josh. We'll both be right here."

The morning began to warm up and Arthur went over to open the doors to all three bays. Sunlight spilled into the bays and the brand new tire on the spare mount of the pick-up truck was a shiny black against the dull and sun faded green paint of his truck. He opened the passenger side door and carefully hung his uniform on the hook behind the seat. He put the sea-bag on the floor, opened the top of it and took out his dopp kit. Beneath the kit was an olive drab towel wrapped around a Ka-Bar knife and a Colt 1911 A1 that he had carried in Viet Nam and which he had carefully smuggled back with the help of a quartermaster friend who owed Josh a favor. He placed them on the seat next to his dopp kit.

"Well, look here Eddy. Here's the soldier boy come back from the wars."

Josh did not turn around. He recognized the voice of the younger Hazen boy.

"He looks just as puny as he did before he left, don't he?" The older brother laughed.

"I reckon this is a good time to finish up some unfinished business with soldier boy." The younger of the two was moving slowly toward Josh. "You do remember that day down at the Red Flame, don't you, soldier boy?"

"Oh, leave him alone, Billy. He's prob'ly fixin' to make up for lost time with that little chili pepper he left behind." His older brother Eddy called out.

"No, no. This'd be a good time to finish up what he started down at the Red Flame."

Josh kept his back turned to the brothers. He ejected the magazine from the .45 and racked the slide, the ejected round fell onto the seat. He locked the slide back and put the ejected round into the magazine then slipped the magazine back into the pistol, thumbed the slide hold lever down and felt the powerful recoil spring send the top round in the magazine into battery. He pushed the thumb safety up and placed the pistol on top of the towel. He heard the Hazen boys' voices but was not aware of what they were saying. He picked up the K-Bar knife and slipped it out of its scabbard and decided on his next move. He turned slowly to face the brothers, with the pistol in his left hand the Ka-Bar in his right.

The brothers looked at the pistol and the knife with alarm. Josh noticed that the younger of the two had stepped over the hydraulic lift and was closest to him. He put the pistol back on the seat of this truck, turned back toward the youngest brother and took two quick steps toward him. He held the knife low, his intention was to deal with the nearest brother first by coming in low and fast into his belly and then he would deal with the bigger, older brother.

As Josh moved toward him with the knife, Billy began to quickly back up and tripped over the hydraulic lift, falling on his back. Josh was on him in an instant, the point of his knife pressing against the skin of Billy's throat.

"You tell your brother to back out of the garage to the driveway. Tell him!"

"Eddy, back up!"

Old man Pierce and Arthur stood just inside the bay staring at Josh whose right hand held the knife at Billy's throat.

"If I ever see you two again, I will kill you." Josh's voice was low and calm. "I will kill you without a thought. Do you understand?"

"I understand." Billy was afraid to nod his head because the point of Josh's knife was digging into his throat.

Josh waited a second or two and then took the Ka-bar away from Billy's throat and turned it so the blade pointed up and then brought the butt of the knife swiftly down on the bridge of Billy's nose. Billy screamed and Josh got up quickly as blood shot out from Billy's nose. The older brother looked on in shock as Billy slowly got up and holding both hands to his face walked quickly out of the garage.

Josh stood holding the knife at his side, the tip of its blade pointing toward the brothers and watched as they got into their car and pulled out onto Main Street, heading south. "Josh!" Mr. Pierce walked over to him. "We got us a new deputy now and he ain't the Lord's brightest creature but worse'n that, he ain't got a sense of humor. He's helping out down in the south county today but will be back this evenin'. I doubt those two boys will complain and me and Arthur couldn't really see what happened but there's a bunch of folks across the street at the drug store saw it and one of them is Luke. So most likely the telling of what happened in my garage is already on its way around the valley."

Josh walked over to the water hose and began washing the blood off the knife and his hands.

"Folks been complainin' 'bout those two East Texas cedar choppers for a while but the new deputy says if they ain't broke the law, then he can't do nothin' 'bout 'em. I'm no lawyer but I reckon what you just done would fit our new deputy's idea of breakin' the law. God, I wish old Eight-ten was back!"

Josh went over to his truck and carefully dried the blade of his knife with the towel and then put it back in its scabbard. He put everything back into the sea-bag and turned to Mr. Pierce and Arthur.

"I want to thank you for taking care of my truck and for the offer of a job. I feel like I gotta pay somethin' for the engine overhaul and everything."

"No, Josh. You don't owe nothin'. We did use the truck and so we're even. You take care of yourself and if you ever need anything you be sure and let me know." He shook Josh's hand and went back to his office.

Josh took the water bag from the bed of the pick-up and went over to the water hose on the island.

"Here now, Josh. You don't wanna fill it with that well water. We got some distilled water in the office. I'll fill it for you while you get the truck out." Arthur took the bag and went into the office.

Josh checked the oil, belts and tires on the pick-up, then pulled it out of the service bay. Arthur came out of the office with the full water bag and two quarts of thirty weight motor oil.

"By God, Josh, it was a pure delight watching you settle that little bastard's hash, but I'd watch my back real close, 'cause them two will surely try to back shoot you."

"Thanks for everything, Arthur." Josh shook his hand.

Sue Ann was behind the counter at the Lone Star Cafe and watched as Josh came in the front door. There were two farmers in a booth drinking coffee. They nodded greetings as Josh walked past them to the counter.

"So the stories are true! Old Josh *is* back in town. She came around the counter and gave Josh a long, slow hug.

"Howdy, Sue Ann." He grinned. Can a fella get a cheese-burger and some fries in this place?"

Sue Ann sat on the stool next to his and smoked a cigarette as she watched him eat his meal.

"I'm still pissed that you never came to say goodbye. I don't care that you skipped out on the graduation ceremonies and that you slipped out of town to join the Marines, but by God, I thought I'd at least get a goodbye kiss. Not only that but you broke little Roble's heart. She came askin' me if I knew where you went to so I told her what Bobby told me since he was the only one that knew. I'm tellin' you, Josh, that little gal was fonder of you than you knew."

"Where is she now?" He ate the last of the potatoes.

"She got a scholarship and is down in Austin at the University studyin' somethin' to do with medicine. You're a damn fool, Josh. She is a real keeper."

"Yeah, I know." He sipped at his coffee.

"Until the day she left for Austin, she would come in regular like and ask if I had heard from you." She frowned. "You need to know, Josh, that you can't treat women like that. You can't leave them wondering, 'specially not one like her! I know you're a big boy and are not afraid of *anything* or *anyone* but I'm thinking that you were afraid of tellin' her goodbye." She crushed out her cigarette in the ashtray that advertised Lone Star beer and then went around the counter to grab the coffee pot and refill his cup.

Josh sipped his coffee and stared at the wall behind the counter.

"I wasn't afraid. . . well, hell I might have been, I don't know. I know I was kinda upset that it didn't look like anything was workin' out for me. I mean, Missy, well, you know about her and Roble, well she was set on leavin' too and I didn't want to hang around here feelin' that big empty feeling...and well..." His voice faded off and he looked straight ahead at the wall.

"Things not workin' out for you? Well, Cowboy, it appears that you could have done somethin' your own self to help the situation. As far as Missy, that's best over with as I have told you before. But don't you reckon you coulda talked to Roble about your plans?"

Josh was quiet, trying to absorb what Sue Ann was saying.

"I reckon you're right, Sue Ann. I'm just not good at talking about that stuff."

Sue Ann decided she had been tough on him long enough. "It's okay, Josh, if you have much more to do with us girls, you'll learn how." She reached over and covered his hand with hers. "Ain't none of my business but if I was you, I'd drop by and say howdy to Roble's mama and papa. They're real proud about you joinin' up and besides her mama will know how to get in touch with Roble. That is, if you want to."

"Oh, yeah. I do want to." He turned and looked into Sue Ann's eyes.

"Well, by God, that's a start! Now you get your ass out to old Señor Gonzalez's place and get this thing goin' again."

Josh reached for his billfold and Sue Ann gave him a withering look. "Don't you even think about it."

"Thanks, Sue Ann." He finished his coffee.

"Want another?" She held up the pot.

"No thanks. I'd best be goin', but I did want to ask you 'bout Rip and Bobby."

"Well Bobby is down in Houston at some cancer hospital and I hear that he's doin' a lot better and they plan to send him home next month. He'll be stayin' with some kin in El Paso until he's well enough to come back here. It looks like they caught the cancer in time and he's whipped it. Rip is drying out at a Veteran's hospital in San Antonio. He's gettin' better too. He actually wrote me twice. I'm keeping Achilles, old Dan's dog, while Rip is in the hospital. He tells me he ain't never goin' to drink again."

"Can you give me the name of the hospital? If I'm down that way I'll stop in and see him."

Sue Ann wrote the address on a napkin.

"San Antonio's not that far from Austin." She smiled.

"Don't know when I'll see you again but thanks for every-thing." Josh reached out to shake her hand but Sue Ann came around the counter and hugged him tight and held him long enough to get the attention of the two farmers. She watched as he opened the front door and stepped outside and thought: "I'm glad you're back safe and sound, Joshua."

Three mornings a week Marisol Gonzalez saddled her favor-ite mare and rode the five miles to visit her sister-in-law and they would spend several hours drinking coffee and discussing the business of their respective ranches, thoroughbred horses and her favorite subject, Teresa's daughter and Marisol's god-daughter, Roble.

Marisol sat at the kitchen table and watched her sister turn tortillas on the comal.

"I have never understood why you refuse to let the cook do that. Why do you even employ her if you still insist on mak-ing tortillas every morning just like Mama did?"

"Perhaps that is the reason. Tradition?" She carefully re-moved the tortilla from the comal and added it to the stack wrapped in a kitchen towel.

"One of the hands said El Huerfano is back and that he was in a fight this morning." She watched for a reaction from her sister-in-law but Teresa did not react, just removed another tor-tilla from the comal.

"Josh is back?" Teresa asked quietly.

"Yes and no doubt will be out here looking for Roble before the day is too old. Damn! Why could he not have stayed gone. He is not the one for my god-daughter."

"I am afraid your god-daughter does not agree with you." Teresa smiled.

"He has no prospects, he has no family, he has no education. He has nothing to offer. He is and always will be, "el pobre Huerfano."

"I agree with you that he has none of those things but he is a hard worker, he is honest and your god-daughter is in love with him."

"I know," Marisol sighed. "But he will be happy to spend the rest of his days working livestock, horseback every day. How does that match up with Roble who wants a better life? A profession in medicine. Think of it, Teresa. Our Roble, a surgeon! Her independence is important to me and I can't see her tied town to a ranch tending to him and horses and cattle every day."

Teresa knew better than anyone the futility of arguing with her head-strong sister-in-law. She would never remind her that in all her life Marisol never found a man strong enough to put up with her and how at times the bitterness showed through and how Marisol was tied down to her ranch more than anyone in the family.

"I have faith that Roble and Josh will, in the end, decide what will become of them. If it is to be then it will be and neither you nor I will have much influence on their feelings for each other or their plans, if any, for the future."

Marisol got up from the table. "I better be getting back. One of my favorite mares is ready to foal and I must be there to see that the idiots I have working for me don't screw it up."

"Don't forget the tortillas." Teresa picked up a dish wrapped in a tea towel.

Teresa walked out with her and held the tortillas while Marisol swung herself up into the saddle. She handed them up to her and Marisol who still had the eyes of her youth looked to the south where the road came off a small rise.

"See, I told you." She pointed to a rooster tail of dust on the road. "El Huerfano." She nudged the mare in the flanks and rode off to her ranch.

Josh sat at the kitchen table while Mrs. Gonzales put a cup of coffee and some pan dulce in front of him.

"It's good to see you, Josh." She smiled at him. Roble had inherited her mother's smiling eyes and it only reminded him of how much he had missed her.

"It's good to be back, ma'am."

The cook stuck her head into the kitchen from the formal dining room but Teresa dismissed her with a look and a small movement of her hand.

"My daughter wanted to write to you but she did not have your address. No one had your address." Mrs. Gonzalez and her daughter shared a direct manner of speaking.

"No, ma'am." He looked away.

"What will you do now that you are back?"

"I'm not sure, ma'am, thought I'd look for work."

"And Roble? Do you plan to see her?"

He did not reply but just looked at her. She caught the confusion and a bit of sadness in him and immediately regretted her question.

"Look, Josh, it is none of my business and I would never pretend to speak for Roble but she loves you and has missed you very much. She talked about you every day until it was clear to her that you may be gone for good and I could tell even in her silence she still thought about you every day. She is working hard at school. She wants to be a doctor and there is no doubt in our minds that she will be one." Josh did not respond but stared into his coffee. "Do you have a job or an offer of one?"

"No, ma'am."

"Then I suggest you go see her in Austin and start over with her. I also suggest you do not dwell on whatever happened between you two but just go right ahead and start a new beginning."

Josh nodded and sipped at his coffee. The pan dulce was untouched. Teresa watched him and wondered if he could ever be the same young man she had known before he went away to the war. The news about his fight in town disturbed her and she thought of her brother, Candido, who came back from the Pacific in World War Two and was never quite the same again.

"Did you have breakfast?"

He looked up but the look on his face told her that he did not really know the answer to her question.

"Let me make you something for the road." She got up and went over to the stove. She put a cast-iron skillet on the grate and went over to the refrigerator and got out some eggs and chorizo. His voice surprised her.

"I reckon I'll go down to Austin and find Roble and do what you said. And then I reckon I'll visit Rip at the hospital in San Antonio. I hear that he's been sick." His voice became stronger, more determined. "I missed Roble every day I was gone, Mrs. Gonzalez. I thought about her all the time and dreamed about her at night and I wanted to talk with her and tell her about my life and ask her about hers but I'm not much good at writing letters. I mean, I must have written hundreds of them in my mind. I just never put them on paper."

Teresa felt a relief and kept her face to the stove so he couldn't see the tears form in her eyes.

"How long has it been since you had chorizo for breakfast?" She asked.

"A long time. A real long time."

She peeled the skin from the chorizo and put it in the skillet and grabbed half a dozen eggs from the sideboard. She drained off some of the grease from the sausage and put the scrambled egg mixture and refried beans into the skillet. The smell of the chorizo frying in the skillet and the fresh tortillas warmed the kitchen and her soul with hope for the quiet young man who sat at her kitchen table.

They talked for a while about horses and ranch work and then after a while she packed six burritos for him in waxed paper, put them in a paper sack and handed them to Josh.

"Nicolas will be sorry he missed you. He is in Marfa looking over a short-horn bull."

"Please give him my regards." They walked out of the kitchen to Josh's pick-up truck.

"Come here, Josh."

He walked over to her and she reached up with her right thumb and made the sign of the cross on his forehead.

"Vaya con bendigas de Dios." She said and then she hugged him close.

He took the back roads south of town and stopped at the bottom of the mesa next to an old loading chute. The wood of the pens was weathered and broken and the slats of the chute were all gone. He reached over and opened his seabag. He took out the Ka-Bar and pistol. He removed the KaBar from its scabbard and cut a piece off the olive drab towel that had been wrapped around the pistol. He put the scabbard back in his sea-bag and wrapped the knife carefully in the piece of towel and placed it inside his right boot top. He wrapped the pistol in the remaining piece of towel and placed it on the seat next to him.

He got out of the truck and walked around the holding pens checking the feel of the knife in his boot. He stopped at where the rear gate had been and remembered gathering cows and bringing them to these pens. It was not that long ago but the pens and loading chute looked as if they had not been used in at least fifty years. He stamped his right foot on the ground to settle the knife and walked over and got into his truck.

He grabbed a burrito and opened the waxed paper wrapping and the warm spicy smell of chorizo made his mouth water. After the first bite he wolfed the rest down quickly and reached for another. He forced himself to eat more slowly since he knew he was capable of eating all six at one sitting. He had four burritos and a bag full of sweet water which was enough to last all day. He would save two of the burritos for supper. The aroma of chorizo filled him with good memories and he began to think that he was on his way to understanding what Roble wanted to do with her life and hoped she had not changed her mind about him.

He turned the key, put his right foot on the starter, turned the engine over and listened to it idle for a moment before pulling out and away from the pens. He headed in the direction of a back road that would bring him out onto the main highway just west of the salt flats.

He would try to make it to Alpine before dark.

ABOUT THE AUTHOR

The Author was raised in far West Texas and five genera-
tions of his family are in their final resting place here.
His great grandfather is buried in Concordia Cemetery
in El Paso, Texas within spitting distance of the grave of
John Wesley Hardin. He has great admiration and
respect for the hardy folks who settled and thrived in this part
of Texas.